I WAS ON THE **WRONG BEAR**

I WAS ON THE

WRONG BEAR

Edited by Vaughn Ward

Bowman Books
The Greenfield Review Press
Greenfield Center, N.Y. 12833

ISBN 0-912678-84-4
LIBRARY OF CONGRESS #91-76638

FIRST EDITION

Second Printing 1997
Third Printing 2002

Bowman Books #5

Bowman Books is an imprint of
The Greenfield Review Press. All of the volumes in this
series are devoted to the contemporary tellings of
traditional tales.

The Greenfield Review Press
Two Middle Grove Road
Greenfield Center, N.Y. 12833

Printed in the United States of America

These tellings are Harvey's gift to

      Bill Smith, Joe Bruchac, and Vaughn Ward
      for their encouragement;

      Deborah Delaney
      for her joyous illustrations.

Vaughn's work is for

      Harvey and his family;

      those incorrigible boys in the Liars' Club
      who keep her humble;

      her Texas uncles, Beauford McWilliams
      and Horace Ramsey,
      who tell some big ones themselves.

Contents

INTRODUCTION

If I'd kept on tellin' the truth, I'd never have gotten into these things! You get in the right group and everyone adds something. . . . If people laugh, they're not mad, they're not cryin'. They're gonna be feelin' better.

Harvey Carr

Harvey Carr is the representative northern woodsman. He was born in Watson, Saskatchewan, in 1917. His father was from Oswego County, New York, and his mother, from Southern Ontario. Harvey's father ran a livery, the local meeting place for good talk. As a boy, Harvey broke Shetland ponies. They were ". . . mean," he remembered,

> . . . one kicked me in the stomach with both hind feet and knocked me cold. I didn't tell anyone. I was afraid they wouldn't let me do it any more.

The woodsman's off-handed toughness already was part of his character.

Carr's father also worked in the woods. As soon as he was old enough, Harvey, who claims to be the "only one in his family who didn't have a brother," went along to watch. He helped his dad until he ". . . got more experience and bigger. I got more and more practice until I got to be a lumber jack." His dad would ". . . throw in a story any time he'd see fit."

Harvey's mother told ". . . a few other stories," including at least one old world magic tale. His grandfather, who was English and Irish, was

> . . . quite a storyteller in his time. And he was tough. "If you get lame from chopping wood," he'd say, "the best thing to do is go out and chop some wood." And he's right. You know, if you're doing something and you get lamed up — something you're not used to — and you get lamed up, go back and do some more. Not too much, but use those muscles again.

As a woodsman, Carr "bounced around wherever there was trees." He has worked at many of the Adirondack live-in lumber camps, including one where the men walked more than eight miles to get into camp. He worked as a guide until he decided he ". . . liked to hunt and fish too much to spoil it by guiding."

Harvey saved his money from working in the woods and graduated from electrician's school in Chicago. Although he did very well, that career was cut short by World War II. He went to radio school in the Army before becoming a paratrooper in the 101st Airborne. In addition to the military applications of this skill, Harvey sent his sweetheart, Mary McGraw, letters in Morse Code, which she knew because she had ". . . taken it in Girl Scouts"! Mary McGraw and Harvey Carr were married in Fort Benning, Georgia, on September 19, 1943, three days after Harvey's birthday. The same week, he took his requisite five parachute jumps. Getting married, he is fond of saying, was ". . . the longest jump of all." Harvey and Mary are very proud of their children: Mary, Laura, John, David, Larry (deceased), their eight grandchildren and one great-grandchild.

After four and a half years as a paratrooper, Harvey Carr ". . . needed to get back to the woods." He worked in the woods for four and a half years and then went to work for the Tree Preservation Company. By the time of his retirement, twenty-three years later, he was the manager of crews for New York State.

Harvey, Mary, and Sparky Carr live in Blue Mountain Lake, where Harvey has taught fishing classes to children at the local arts center and served as chairman of the Board of Fire Commissioners. When the Hochschild family was setting up the Adirondack Museum, it was Harvey who brought the cabin of Noah John Rondeau, the famous Adirondack hermit, out of the woods and set it up at the museum. He also draws upon his incredibly exact memory to advise curators on technicalities of hand logging. When he described the process of icing roads for ". . . sleigh hauling," I could see what a help he had been:

> . . . . *The roads were hard-packed snow, and they packed 'em and they rolled 'em some and then they'd snowplow. They'd draw with about two to three teams of horses to get the snow packed down and pounded down. After you once got it flattened and started hauling, you had to go with a sleigh full of logs. . . . The winter of 1939–1940, I was icing the roads. [We used] what they called a* water sprinkler; *they've got one up to the museum. It was a big truck and you built a tank out of boards. Then you put the tar paper on the*

inside and then you put another layer of boards on the inside. You know, it waterproofed pretty good. It would take, oh, probably 1000 gallons of water. It's big, box-like. In the back there were a couple of holes two inches in diameter in the bottom of the tank. Wooden plugs would fit into them on a little chain, so you wouldn't drop them in the water or something. . . . They come straight back over each runner, spaced just right. So you just knock those plugs out and start and go right on down the road and you leave that water on top of the track — if it's good and cold. It's gotta be below zero or it won't work well.

Oh, I made money, running [the water sprinkler] at night and loading pulpwood in the daytime. . . . They'd ice the roads wherever it was flat, 'cause that would make it that much firmer. Even the good, hard-packed snow will sag with the runners. So you're more or less pulling your load uphill all the while. See what I mean? The haul with a big load of logs on, and the weight, and the road would sag as the sleigh went over it. That's what the icin' was for — to make it solid enough so it wouldn't sag. And, if it sagged, it's like climbin' up a little hill all the while. . . .

Woodsmen recognize each other by their stories. When the well-known St. Lawrence County basket maker and woodsman, Bill Smith, was working at the Adirondack Museum a number of years ago, Harvey was whittling chains on the porch. Harvey recalls:

Bill said, "You used to do quite a lot of logging."
I said, "Yes, I did."
Bill said, "How'd you like it?"
I said, "I did. I really enjoyed it. You know, outdoors, fresh air and exercise. And then I told him the story about drivin' the logs back upstream.
He kind of looked at me and he said, "I think that guy's a liar!"

When Bill Smith, Eliot Older, and I were dreaming up the Liars' Club, Bill was certain. "Harvey has to be there. He's the best of the old-time lumberjacks. I'll talk to him." The first meeting of the Adirondack Liars' Club (a performance group of traditional tall tale masters) was at the Methodist Church in Middle Grove, New York, in October of 1987, and Harvey was there. It was his first public performance, and our first meeting. With the wicked gleam I've come to love and distrust, he set me up with his favorite trick: He played the simpleton until *I* said something dumb! Five years later, he could tell me exactly what I had said. It occurs to me that this man may have remembered, and warehoused for reworking, every story he has ever heard.

When Harvey went out from Blue Mountain Lake to share these stories with a wider audience, he went as a representative of all the cronies at all the corner stores and bars in the Adirondacks. He has carried the fine art of woods talk to audiences all over upstate New York, including appearances at Crary Mills, St. Lawrence County; at four Old Songs Festivals in Altamont, Albany County; at the Washington County Fair. When he left for his first big public performance, his buddies gave him his prized Liars' Club sweatshirt, ". . . as a going-away present." The instant joke about the French Foreign Legion cuts off any mush. They know. Harvey knows.

Vaughn Ward
Rexford, New York
November 1991

Harvey Carr died on December 17, 1991, after a long and lucid struggle with cancer. He enjoyed until the very end, giving me the information on icing the roads the *same day* he went to the hospital for the last time. This book is epitaph and eulogy, a guarantee that, as Joe Bruchac said, " . . . moments of laughter and wonder that spring from the spirit have not been lost to the world . . ."

HELLO,
I'M HARVEY CARR

Hello there! Hi everybody. I'm Harvey Carr, live right here in Blue Mountain Lake. Beautiful little town. I kinda live up in the suburbs here now, it's about three hundred yards from where we are right now. But it's a nice little town, really nice. Quiet in the winter, not dead, but quiet sometimes. Every once in a while we perk it up, we liven things up a little bit. I don't know if you've noticed my sweatshirt or not—"Liar's Club," it says—doesn't show up very well. Some of my buddies bought it for me for a goin' away present. I've got another program coming up here in a couple of weeks up in Crary Mills, up near Potsdam and my buddies gave it to me for a goin' away present. They also gave me a life membership in the French Foreign Legion. Only problem was that they made me promise not to come back home again.

"You get tellin' stories over in the hunting camp, or lumber camp, or over in the coffee shop. One story will lead to another . . . " Harvey heard stories about frozen flames around his father's livery ". . . when I was a little kid in Saskatchewan." The brag about the extreme cold is easy for anyone in the north country to believe. Whose teeth haven't "chattered until they were almost lame"? Wait. These are false teeth taking on their own life. This mechanical silly began with Mary's uncle, Jim Davey:

> . . . .He was up here. He was 91 or 92 years old. I told him a story about it bein' . . . too cold, and he said, "Like the teeth chatterin' in the pocket," which is in itself a good, quickie story. But I said to myself, "Sounds like room for improvement there. I'll do something with it."

The ratio of hot to cold in these anecdotes is the truth about North Country climate. The joke about the dog and the rabbit — sometimes a fox replaces the dog — has been collected from Alberta to Arizona, and in some parts of Europe. The one about frozen flames/words was first recorded in ancient Greece. In eighteenth century England, it appeared in Addison and Steele's tabloid, The Tatler. I asked Harvey how he thought these old jokes and stories made their way to the north woods. "Some joker," he declared as if he had been thinking about how stories travel, "some joker took it, and customized it, and remodeled it. He remade it to fit the Adirondacks."

1

MODERN NOW

Yep, it's a pretty nice little town up here. Gettin' pretty modern now. We've got village water and we've got electric lights and we've got sidewalks and the streets are paved and it is getting pretty modern now. Years ago, of course, we didn't have all these modern conveniences, but we still got along. We did the best we could. A buddy of mine came up from the city one day. He was goin' to spend two or three days here in the Adirondacks with me and we sat at the kitchen table visiting and he said, "Say Harvey, can I use your bathroom?"

I said, "Well, we don't rightly have a bathroom. We got an outhouse out here. That works pretty good."

So I gave him a flashlight; it was dark out. Gave him the flashlight and showed him the trail, a nice little trail.

"Shoot right up this trail oh, about a hundred yards," I said, "and on your right you'll see a little building and that's the outhouse."

So, away he went. Well, I sat there and he'd been gone 15 to 20 minutes and he didn't come back. I wondered if something happened to old Joe, but I couldn't figure out how anything could happen because it is a good trail and he had a flashlight and everything. But, I said to

myself, "I'd better go up and check." I took another flashlight and up the trail I went. I got up to the outhouse and I hollered and he wasn't there. I got kind of worried about him then, so I walked up the trail a little further and I hollered again. And I could hear a weak, little "Help!" I went up further, and what it was, he missed the outhouse and he went and fell in the well. I looked down the well and Old Joe was down in there, sloshing around.

I said, "Joe, are you O.K.?"

He said, "Well, I am so far but for God's sake don't flush this thing till I get out of here!"

HOT AND COLD, BUT NOTHING EXTREME

We got some pretty good weather up here. Oh, it gets kind of hot sometimes, nothing really severe, but it does get kind of hot. In fact, a week ago here I went up the trail up back of the house here, just hiking through the woods and I saw a fox chasing a rabbit. It was so hot they were both walking.

It got pretty cold up here last winter. It got down to about zero. Of course, that was in the kitchen. I didn't mind the cold weather. I was going to take a hike to Rock Pond and back and it got cold and kept getting colder and colder. It got so cold my teeth were chattering and then chattered and chattered until my jaws got lame. I couldn't put up with that so I took my teeth out (I wear dentures, of course) and put them in my hip pocket and they kept right on chattering. It was cold and I didn't want to stop, so I kept on going and those false teeth kept on chattering and chattering. First they bit me a couple or three times a little bit, then they chewed a hole right through the pants pocket and they dropped right into the snow. We had a foot and a half of light snow on, and I couldn't find them.

I had to go back the next spring after the

snow all went off and sure enough I found them. They showed up pretty good on the bare ground. And when I found them they were still chattering.

Yes, it got pretty cold. I guess it was the same day it was zero in the kitchen that I decided to go outside and build a bonfire and get warm. I got the fire going and I got the flames coming up there pretty good and it kept getting colder and colder and finally it got so cold that it froze the flames right in mid-air. That wasn't kicking off any heat and I said "What am I going to do now?." So I went down to the house and I got the food grinder. I brought that up there and I ground those flames right up into a powder and I ran home and put them right in the freezer. You know, that made the best red pepper I ever had in my life!

It does get pretty cold and in the late fall when it gets cold, it gets cold fast. A year ago, a little later than this, I was out water skiing and it turned cold and boy, did the temperature drop! Right down to about 20 below zero in a matter of minutes. It got so cold it froze the boat right in the water and froze me right in the ice in my skis. What they had to do, they had to bring a snowmobile in from town and an axe to chop the boat loose and chop my skis loose. My feet were so frozen to the skis so they had to ski me all the way back to shore with the snowmobile.

Harvey's bear stories are great-great grandchildren of European tales in which the hero overcomes the ogre through magic or superhuman strength. "Bruno" features a hero so strong, so brave, and so drunk, that he can ride a wild bear without noticing anything unusual — a feat only a little beyond a day's work for Adirondack men! Like many old stories, this has moved between print and oral circulation with some regularity. Print versions appeared in the Crockett Almanacs, popular in the nineteenth and early twentieth centuries, and in the Paul Bunyan cycle. Similar stories have been collected from oral sources in New Mexico and in Alberta. "Speakin' of Bears" plays with the hero's escape through bluffing. Harvey is at his best here, supplying plenty of concrete detail as a set-up. The story about the hero who miraculously escapes from a mother bear has cousins in many parts of the United Sates and in Estonia. "In the Bear Den" is distantly related to the fairy tale The Seven Sleepers, to Rip Van Winkle, to marvel journeys to another world through a pit entrance, to accounts of a magical, shrinking person, and to narratives involving supernatural time lapses — all standard features of old world marchen, or fairy tales. The hero-who-starves-in-his-own-story motif is distinctly tall tale American.

BRUNO

Blue Mountain Lake is a great little town. We have a lot of fun. Used to have a little local tavern here, Wheeler's Restaurant, probably some of you folks remember that. We used to go down there and it was a real friendly little pub and we had a lot of fun. Well, I used to go down every pay day and I had my beer and so on, enough for me and maybe for a couple of other fellows who weren't there, and I would get pretty tipsy. I only lived about 400 yards from the tavern but I would have to walk about four miles before I got home, so I had this little bear cub. I raised him from a cub and trained him so that I could get on his back and just ride him home.

He got to be a pretty good-size bear. He got up to be, oh, about 300 to 400 pounds and I had him pretty well trained. I'd take him down to Wheeler's with me, but I had to leave him outside because there is a sign on the door that says "No Bare Feet" and he had four of them. He would curl up in Eddie's flower bed and I would take him out a couple of soda pops and a candy bar and leave him there while I went in and had my beer. And that went on good.

Well, I came out one night pretty tipsy and I just tickled his ear and I said, "O.K. Bruno,

let's go home." Boy, he snarled at me and I said, "Bruno, come on now, be a good bear. We want to go home now." And I reached out to pet him and he snapped at me again. Well, then I got a little bit peeved and I had to cuff him up a little bit. We had quite a go-around there and I cuffed him up pretty good. Finally, I got him calmed down and I hopped on his back and everything worked good. He brought me right home just like a good bear should. Just as I was getting off his back, I looked around back behind the house and there lay Bruno sound asleep. I was on the wrong bear!

SPEAKIN' OF BEARS

There are quite a few bear up in this country. We've got a hunting camp on top of Little Blue Mountain and we were up there, four or five of us. It was a real nasty day, half rain, half snow and almost freezing out and a pretty miserable day, but being a real dedicated hunter I wanted to go hunting. All of the rest of the boys would rather stay in camp and have a beer or two and play cards or something. I couldn't talk them into going hunting so I went out alone. I got way up into the woods there and I was tippy-toeing along like you are supposed to when you're hunting. I was hunting for deer or bear, either one. I looked up and here is a big old bear. So I pulled up real careful-like and took dead center on him and I shot. I pretty near missed him. All I did, I just nicked him in the ear, just enough to make him mad. Well, he took after me and we started running. Well, I dropped the rifle. I didn't have time to shoot anyway and I could run faster without it and I headed right for camp. It was quite a ways there, and I was kind of getting out of breath but I got to camp. Just as I stepped up on the door step and turned the door knob I tripped and fell down. Well, the old bear was going so fast, that he went right

into the camp right over the top of me. So I got up and closed the door from the outside and I hollered, "You fellas take care of that one and I'll go and get another one."

Speakin' of bears, I went to the Washington County Fair last year. We had a little program down there and I was wandering around to look at everything and here is a cage out in the middle of the fair grounds with a bear in it. He was a pretty good size, a 300-pound black bear and I was looking at him and there's this beautiful little gal. She comes up all dressed up in silver and she opens the cage and she walks right in and closes the door. The old bear walks over to her and rears right up and puts his arms and paws right around her shoulders and he nibbles on her ear a little and licks her cheek. This was really a pretty good show.

My buddy was standing there with me and he said, "Boy, Harve, you wouldn' t dare to do that, would you?"

And I said, "The hell I wouldn't. You just get that damn bear out of there."

I have had quite a few experiences with bear. I was out hunting one day and I looked and I saw a big, great big old stub about that big around and it was broken off up there about 15 feet. I could see it was hollow and I looked and there were claw marks all over it. So, I was kind of curious to see what was up in there. So I set my rifle down and I shimmied up a little tree beside the stub and I looked in there and there is two of the cutest little bear

13

cubs you ever saw in your life. Oh, they were cute. So, I was goin' to take them home with me and tame them like I did Old Bruno. I took my belt off and I took my shoelaces off, figuring I could tie up their feet and take them home with me and tame them. So, I shimmied up and down inside and I was hasseling around with them. I wasn't getting along too bad, when all of a sudden I looked and it got dark. I looked up and here's old Ma Bear coming right down the stub, stern end first, right on top of me. "Man, I'm a goner now," I thought. "The rifle is outside and so I guess I'm a goner." Well, I had my hunting knife there so the only thing I could do, I waited till she got down close enough and I grabbed her right by the tail and I jabbed her one — right in the rear end. Boy, you talk about a couple of homesick angels going up, we went up over the stub like a streak. We got up out of there and she jumped off to the left and I jumped off to the right. Luckily that's where my rifle was and I grabbed my rifle and away I went. I haven't monkeyed with a bear cub since.

IN THE BEAR DEN

I was out hunting right out back here, right here out of Blue Mountain Lake, back over the ridge and up on Blue Ridge, pretty good hunting country. I was tip-toeing along up there and all of a sudden the ground dropped from under me. Down I went. I must've went down, oh, 20 or 25 feet. What it was, I guess, was I dropped right through a crevice in a rock and right down through, right down the bottom. I hit bottom and I heard a little whuff! or something there, but I wasn't sure just what it was. It kind of knocked the wind out of me and I just sat there for a while. But when I got so I could see a little better, there was a great big old bear laying there sound asleep. He was hibernating. I was in quite a predicament. The tunnel where the bear came into the den was on the other side of the bear from me. There wasn't room to get out around him and, man, if I ever tried to go over the top of that bear he might wake up and tear me right to pieces. "Well," I thought, "I might as well take a little nap." So I curled up and went to sleep. About every three or four days I'd wake up and I'd look. But that old bear was still there and there was nothing else I could do, so I'd go back to sleep again. Well that

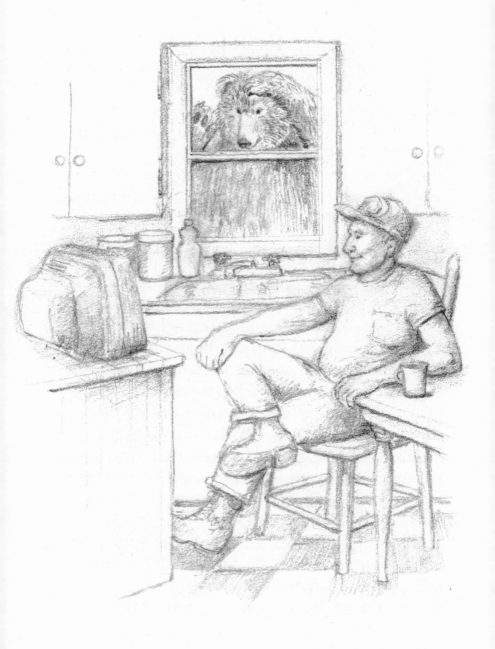

went on till, oh, about the middle of April. Then one day I woke up and I looked and the bear was gone. Boy, that was a relief. I crawled out of there pretty careful-like and looked around. Sure enough, the bear was nowhere in sight. Well, by that time I was feeling pretty hungry. It had been from the middle of November till April.

I said to myself, "Man, the first thing I got to do is get something to eat. Maybe I'll stop at the neighbor's there and get something."

But then I realized I was so hungry, I would eat everything he had in the house and make a disgrace of myself. I couldn't do that, so I decided I'd better go down to the supermarket. I went down to Indian Lake to the supermarket. There's a Grand Union down there and they got one of these new-fangled rubber mats in front of the door, you know the kind. You walk onto it and your weight trips a switch and the door opens. Well, I'd lost so much weight that the doggone door wouldn't even open. You know, I had to wait till another customer came up and stood on there with me before the doors opened. Well, I got in and I got filled up after a while and I don't know if I ever paid them the rest of the food bill or not.

Well, then I thought I better get home. My good wife, Mary, might be worried about me seeing as how I'd been gone about six months. But when I came in she didn't seem to be too upset. She just looked up and said, "Hi Harve, how was the hunting?"

17

Late last fall, it was getting pretty cold and so I sat there in the kitchen one evening watching television. We've got a little black and white TV there in the kitchen, and I was watching that. Then I heard a little bumping noise. I looked out the window and there wass a big old bear. He was leaning right against the window, watching TV.

I thought, "Well I don't mind that, you know, we can both watch it." He was kind of looking over my shoulder but I didn't mind that too much. Well, came the end of that program, whatever it was, I got up and went over to go and change channels to another station and get a different program. Gee, that old bear started pounding on the window. I thought he was going to break it. What in the world is the matter with him? So, anyway, I got up and turned the TV back to the station that had been on before. Then I realized what it was. "Gentle Ben" was just coming on and he wanted to watch it.

*"Hembal Salve's" accurate information about bal-
sam and hemlock, which are used for home remedies,
lulls us to accept the mixed-category magic that his
salve can mend animal, mineral and vegetable. Stories
about magic salves, healing springs, and other magic
remedies are told in Europe. They tell about a healing
spring that fixed up a wolf who had been separated
from his tail in New Jersey, Iowa, and Arkansas. Harvey's version is from his mother, who called it "The
Magic Salve."*

*Subtle details of what is unsaid are Harvey's trade-
mark. He delights in unstated absurdities: "Imagine,"
he chuckled to me, "imagine even considering hitting
your foot with an ax more than once!" For a lesser
artist, this bit of comic rigidity might have been the
whole joke: Harvey buries it in a passing compound
sentence!*

HEMBAL SALVE

Well, I have to tell you a little bit about my dog. I used to have a dog years ago here, oh, about 30 years ago when I was just a teenager and he was quite a dog. Times were kind of rough right then and we didn't have the money to buy anything anything like cloverine salve or rosebud salve. So I decided to make my own. What I did, I took the inner bark of a hemlock tree and I steeped it just like you would tea. Then I took the balsam pits there, those little bubbles, you know, on the outside of a balsam tree and I mixed them up with that hemlock juice. I called it *Hembal Salve*.

It worked good. One day I was out there in the woods and I cut my foot with the axe. I didn't cut it too bad, I only hit it once. I ran in and I got some of the salve and I put that on. It had healed it up real quickly. Well, I had a cracked axe handle there, cracked, pretty near broke apart, so I rubbed some of the salve on it and it made that handle just as good as new.

It worked pretty good. Anything from a broken window pane to a broken leg, it would cure it. I was out there one day and I was splitting wood. Ol' Spot there, my dog, was out there with me. He kinda wandered around the place there, wagging his tail. I tried to keep him out of the way but he was pretty friendly. I was just cutting the wood and I just brought the axe down and just before it hit the block Ol' Spot wagged his tail right under that axe and I chopped his tail off.

Well now, I felt bad about that. Ol' Spot was whining and yipping and crying a little bit. Then I thought of that *Hembal Salve.* So I ran in and brought it out and rubbed it on the little stub of Spot's tail. He quit whining and yipping and crying and he even started to wag that little stub of a tail. Well, I said, "I guess it's going to be all right." It went on a little while there and, you know, Spot grew a new tail. He even looked better with that long tail anyway.

Next spring I was out doing a little spring cleaning, raking up the chips and saw dust and bark and whatever. Lo and behold, there was Spot's tail. Well, I picked it up. I didn't quite know what to do with it. I didn't know whether to have it bronzed or pickled or what. Then I thought about the *Hembal Salve.* I went in and I got it and I rubbed it on that old tail and it grew a new dog. You know, you couldn't tell those dogs apart.

Carr blackflies act like larger-than-life tall tale heros; the chipmunks, like spoiled grandchildren. Dogs are the hero's companions: they read minds and understand speech. These animals are more like shapeshifters, the tricksters who assume animal forms in ancient stories, than they are like the prey in the münchausen *marvelous hunt stories.*

Thirty-five or forty years ago, Harvey worked in the woods with "an old lumberjack" named Jack Roche, who was ". . . a great one for some of them old stories." Roche had

> . . . an Andy Devine voice. He'd tell a story and everybody'd laugh and he'd turn around and look to see what they were laughin' at. . . . I worked with him there off and on for years. He didn't wear these stories out by tellin' 'em over and over and over again.

Roche is the only person Harvey heard tell the porcupine story.

Beavers may be the perfect tall tale animal hero, as anyone who has lost land or road to beaver ingenuity knows. Harvey told me about the circular beaver dam on Lake Durant, just up the road from his house in Blue Mountain Lake, which drains forty or fifty acres. Then he showed me up in my true colors as a gullible from town:

> "Did you know there's always at least one muskrat livin' in every beaver dam?"
> "No!" (I bit.)
> "Yep. Muskrats are too little to drag logs around, so the beavers have at least one for a timekeeper."

"I take a little here and a little there. . . . and make a story out of it," Harvey went on. As a boy, he hung

22

around his father's livery stable, taking in the stories and the way of telling. He particularly remembers hearing Ty Fair, "an old farmer," and Mike Green, "who was quite a joker."

SPARKY

I guess I have to tell you about the dog I got now, Ol' Sparky. She is quite a dog. She is about three-and-a-half years old now and she is part Labrador and part Siberian and part thoroughbred I guess. She weighs about 80 pounds. She's pretty frisky and pretty fast, but she is kind of awkward. I guess she's got two left feet, but we get along pretty good. She's getting pretty smart. She can't read yet but she has fun looking at the funny papers and she likes to hunt with me. She likes fishing, too. All I have to do if I'm going to go trout fishing or bullhead fishing or something, is pick up my fishing tackle and fish pole and boy, she runs right out and digs worms for me.

I was up at Dunbrook with her one day and fishing in the stream there and I went to change the lures or cut the line off or do something. I used my jackknife and then I stuck it in a log and I went on fishing downstream, oh, a half mile, I guess. I wanted to use my knife again so I reached for it. Then I remembered I'd left it up in that log.

So I said, "Sparky, you want to go up to that log and get my jackknife?"

She just went a little "woof" and away she went. It wasn't more than a couple of minutes and back she come with a knife in her mouth.

I looked at it and said, "Sparky, that isn't my knife. Go get my knife, you know, up on that log."

So away she went again. It wasn't long before she came with another knife. I looked and that wasn't mine, either.

So, I said, "Sparky, go up and get my knife. It's sticking in the log up there and you should remember where I left it."

Away she went. You know, that dog she brought back seven jackknives before she brought mine.

I have to tell you a little bit about how I got Sparky. Went down to the pet shop in Glens Falls there and I got a dog. Boy, it was a beauty. I brought it home and my good wife, Mary, asked me "Say, where did you get the dog? That's beautiful."

"From the pet shop in Glens Falls."

She said, "How much did it cost you?"

"It cost me a thousand dollars."

Then Mary hit the ceiling. She said, "A thousand dollars for a dog, we can't afford that! That's too much money. You take that dog back and get your money back."

So away I went.

When I came back, she says, "Did you get your money back?"

And I said, "Kinda."

She said, "What do you mean, kinda?"

And I said, "Well, I swapped it for two five-hundred dollar cats."

Well, boy, then she did hit the ceiling. So I had to take them cats and get my money back. Then I went down to the animal shelter and got Sparky, the best dog I ever had.

Sparky is quite a dog. She's pretty tough too. Here last fall I was out back here and I was going to blow a stump out of the trail. I got a few sticks of dynamite and I went back and I was digging a hole into the stump to put the dynamite in when Ol' Sparky came up and she ate three or four sticks of that dynamite before I could catch her and get the rest of the dynamite away from her. I was pretty worried about her. That dynamite would probably kill that poor dog, make her awful sick anyway. But it didn't seem to bother her too much. She was pretty perky all day. When it was about nine-thirty or ten o'clock at night I heard quite a racket outside. Sparky, she went to the back door and started jumping up and down and barking and yipping and whining. So, I let her go out. Well, what it was, was a big old bear out there. A big one, 300 pounds I guess. Sparky, she went to chase the bear. She nipped at the bear and the bear cuffed at her and they got into quite a hassle. Boy, they went around and around. What finally happened, is that bear got hold of her and started to squeeze Sparky a little too tight. Then that dynamite blew up! It killed the bear and it blew the wood shed right down, broke about half the windows in the house and, you know, poor Ol' Sparky was lamed up there for about a week.

BLACK FLIES

I'll tell you a little bit about our wildlife up here. We have a pretty good variety of deer and bear and bobcats and coyotes and so on and so forth. Quite a variety of wild life. Last spring we had quite a lot of black flies and they were quite a bother but they sprayed them and then they weren't too bad.

The other day, though, I thought they were back again. I saw what I thought was a swarm of black flies — but it was only black birds bunching up and getting ready to go south. They're about the same size and it's kind of hard to tell them apart.

PORKY

I got an apple tree out back here and it always has nice apples. They are coming along pretty good right now, but last year it was pretty hard to figure out what was going on. There were a lot of apples on there but every day when I went out the apples looked scarcer than they were the day before.

So I kept track of it and the next thing I knew half the apples were gone. I decided to sit watch to see if somebody was stealing them at night. I got a flashlight and I went out and I sat there out of sight watching the apple tree. Well, here came an old porcupine. What he did was he climbed up that apple tree and shook the daylights right out of it until a bunch of apples dropped on the ground. Then he went down and rolled on them. When he got up he had an apple on pretty near every quill. He walked away with about half a bushel at a time. I finally got a few of those apples, but the only way I could keep that porcupine out of there was to stay up all night and chase him away.

CHIPMUNKS

We have some chipmunks here, real tame. They're cute little rascals and in the summer they come right up and eat right out of my hand and climb right up my leg and take peanuts out of my pocket. They got pretty tame, so I was feeding peanuts in the shell and it got so that they would take one in each cheek and take one in their teeth and away they'd go, three at a time after they learned how to carry them that way.

That went on pretty good, until I ran out of peanuts in the shell. But I had a jar of dry-roasted, salt-free peanuts. Of course, chipmunks or any animal, you don't give them any salted peanuts — that'll make them sick. They have to eat dry-roasted, salt-free peanuts. So I put some of them out for them. Well, they picked up a bunch of them and took them and away they went. Pretty soon, though, here came a chipmunk with three peanuts in the shell in his cheek. He brought them over and dropped them right in front of me. Now that he'd seen those shelled peanuts he'd brought back the ones still in the shell and I had to shell them for him.

BEAVERS

Wildlife is really something, really interesting. Never know what they're going to do next. I was up in Dunbrook Mountain there. I worked up there three years one summer cutting logs with a chain saw. Every night when I got done cutting, I'd fill the saw full of gas and chain oil and get all ready for the next morning. Next morning, two or three cranks and away it would go. Well, I came up one morning and I cranked, and I cranked and it wouldn't start. So I checked it all over and it was out of gas.

I said, "Well I forget to fill it up last night."

So I filled it up and away it went. It worked good all day.

That night, I said, "Tonight I am going to be sure to fill it up!"

I filled it up with gas, got it all set and went to camp. Back the next morning, I cranked on it and the same thing, it was out of gas. I decided there must be a leak in the gas tank, or gas line, in the carburetor or somewhere. I checked it all over but I couldn't find any leak.

So, I filled it up anyway and I cut logs all day and it worked good. Well, that night after dinner I decided to go back up. It was quite a ways up the mountain. I got half way up the

mountain and I could hear a chain saw running. It sounded kind of like mine. I sneaked up to where I was cutting logs and I looked. Well sir, there was a couple of beaver and they had that chain saw and they were really going to town with it. They were cutting logs and brush and building themselves a dam. They were having a great time up there.

I was telling a buddy of mine, Brother Blanchard, about it later and he said, "Well, say, they must be pretty clever little animals."

And I said, "Not really, I think they're kind of dumb in a way."

He said, "How do you mean dumb?"

I said, "Well sir, there's five gallons of gas and a lot of chain oil there. If they had filled it up when they got through with it I never would have caught them."

Stories about vines growing so fast that they drag the produce along the ground are known from the Mid-Atlantic to the Southwest. Magic vine stories are found in the Georgia and South Carolina Sea Islands, in the Appalachains, and in England ("Jack and the Beanstalk"). "Great vegetable" stories are popular in rural Scandanavia. In Indiana there is a story about a pumpkin used for a raft. Harvey's amazing memory seems to have banked these one-liners to reset them at just the right, desperate moment:

Last summer my little nine-foot patch must've yielded about two-hundred pounds of zuchinni! People don't trust me anymore during growing season. They always lock their cars [something not otherwise necessary in Blue Mountain Lake]. I told everybody I gave zuchinni to, I said, "Now, don't you pack them in tight together. They gotta have room. . . . They keep growing until you chop 'em up and eat 'em." The zuchinni are a problem. Someone said, "We're gonna have to hire Blanchard with his forklift and dump truck to pick the damn zuchinni." So that's the way that started. And I thought, "I can do better than that!" So I made a canoe.

GARDENING

I got quite a garden over there this year. I had a good one last year too, but I learned a little more about gardening since then. This year when I put in some cucumbers I followed the book right to the letter. Last year I read the instructions that said use so much fertilizer to a square foot of cucumber bed. I decided that if a little bit was good, a lot would be better. I put on a lot of it and those cucumbers grew and grew. That wasn't too bad, but the trouble was that they grew so fast that the vines were dragging the cucumbers right along on the ground and they were all skinned and barked up and I had to go way up into the woods and get them. So this year I cut it down to just the fertilizer you're supposed to have.

And then last year I had quite a zucchini patch. Of course, that zucchini — once it gets growing — there only way you can stop it, is you have to shoot it. So, it was growing, growing along pretty good. I got one there that was getting pretty big and it looked pretty tough. I said, well I don't think I'll eat that one, so I left it just to see how big it would get. It just kept growing and growing and it got up, oh, about twelve foot long and probably four foot in diameter. Well, that was quite a zucchini, quite a squash.

But what was I going to do with it? Well, then I had a thought. I decided to hollow that out and make a dug-out canoe. I sliced the top off it end-ways and I scooped it all out good. Then I put it out and let it dry some and took it down to the lake. I took a couple of paddles with me so I could try it out. I put it in the lake and it floated pretty good. I got into it and it carried me pretty well and I paddled right along.

I was getting along good. But I got over into West Bay, I saw a beaver swimming towards me. So I stopped and watched. He was looking kind of curious and he came right up to me. I thought he was going to let me pet him, but instead he sniffed the canoe and then he took one little bite out of it. Right away he turned around and slapped his tail on the water just like a rifle shot! And here comes seven or eight more beaver. Well, you know, they ate that canoe right out from under me. I had to swim like crazy to get to shore.

This year I got another one, it isn't quite that long but this old zucchini is about ten or eleven feet now and I'm going to do the same thing. I'm going to hollow it out and make another canoe. But I think what I better do this year is one of two things. Either I have to put a 25 horse motor on it so as I can outrun a beaver, or I have to fiberglass the outside of it so they can't eat it.

People who have known Harvey a long time remem-
ber that, as a younger man, he played the harmonica
and told true stories of life in the live-in lumber camps.
Harvey introduced the next section of the tape from
which these stories are transcribed with some tunes on
his "mouth organ," which he played in the bunkhouse
in his younger days.

The use of the harmonica in this particular place is a
mark of Harvey's control of narrative structure: cause
and effect has run amuck. Shape-shifting is out of con-
trol. The troopers are witless. Mary Carr looks like
Mrs. Bunyan's sister. The harmonica plays on, support-
ing the ruse that all this is just the way the Carr house-
hold goes along!

The episode with the egg-stealing snake is a decre-
scendo *from the crazy magic it follows. With a solution*
satisfactory to anyone who has kept chickens, our hero
takes charge.

SPEAKIN' OF CEREAL

I'm not very good on the mouth organ anymore. I got to do a little more practicing. I used to play it pretty good back 30 years ago when I was a teenager, but I haven't played it much since. Well, you know I played the mouth organ before President Roosevelt was elected. So, I practice on it once and a while now. I'm not very good at it yet.

A funny thing happened this other day. I got up in the morning and I had breakfast. I always have a bowl of cereal for breakfast and I feed Ol' Sparky at the same time. So I filled her bowl up and I filled up my bowl and we had our breakfast. Then I got kind of a funny feeling in my stomach and I didn't know what was going on. Before I could stop myself I was out back and I was barking at people that were going by. I chased a cat up a tree and then I went out and I was chasing cars until the troopers came along. They saw me chasing cars so they stopped me and it's a good thing there were two of them in the car. They were going to lock me up, but the one wanted to take me to the dog pound and the other wanted to take me to the Hamilton County Jail. While they were arguing about it I sneaked away and come home and if you think what happened to me

was funny, you should have seen Ol' Sparky trying to play my mouth organ. You know, I'm going to be more careful of mixing up my cereal and dog food from now on.

Speaking of cereal, just the other night, I was carving. I do quite a lot of carving there, mostly carving wooden chains out of a piece of wood. I do that at the kitchen table and it's kind of a clean little hobby. You just pick up the shavings when you get done and it works out pretty well. Well, I swept up all the shavings off the table and had them sitting there in a bowl and my wife came along. She looked at them. She thought it was cereal, so she took it and put some milk and sugar on it and she ate it. Well, she ate it before I knew what was going on. So, then she came over to me and said, "Harvey, that's cereal is pretty good."

I said, "That wasn't cereal, that was wood shavings".

"Oh, well," she said, "next time use sugar pine, it tastes a lot better."

SNAKE STEALING EGGS

We got some pretty good-size snakes up there in this country. Luckily none of them are poisonous, but they get pretty big. This big old spotted adder, he'd come along and steal eggs. I had a few chickens out there and I got a few eggs every day until that old snake started coming in to steal the eggs.

He was pretty sneaky about it and I never could catch him. So I got thinking about it and I thought, "Well I'm going to try something." So what I did, I took a board, oh, an inch board about a foot square. I drilled a hole the size of a quarter in the middle of it and I set that up on edge. Then I took a couple of wooden eggs, the kind that they put in chickens' nests to encourage them to lay. They're about as big around as a half a dollar. I put one on each side of the hole in that board and I caught that snake. What he did, he came up and he swallowed one of those wooden eggs. He didn't know the difference. Then he crawled halfway through the hole and he swallowed the other egg and I had him.

Harvey observes that he's ". . . one of the last of the old-time lumberjacks." Other woodsmen, who know what the natural world will and won't do, are his most appreciative audience. The ability to tell a convincing lie marks the insider; the falling for one, the outsider.

The men at the corner store in Blue Mountain Lake have had plenty to opportunity to practice on "city sports," who hire local guides to direct their hunting and fishing trips. Do they know the difference between upstream and downstream? Try them on the one about the logger and the crooked mill owner. Will they believe what they're told about the weather? "Mud Season" suggests the answer.

These single-motif narratives lead us right across the credibility gap to the bears in the telephone booth. This one, Harvey says,

> . . . dawned on me all of a sudden. It was a cold morning. I stood in the post office. . . . Right directly across the road sits a phone booth. I think somebody was using the phone and they were damn near freezin'. Somebody says, "Hey, it's cold out there." They should have a heater in there." And I said, "Well, they used to have, you know." That was the original — struck right then. I said. "Now, they had to take the heater out. . . ."

Which leads to that odd musing about unemployed lumberjacks in bear suits. Which reminds our hero of a time when he was at risk from a blackberry-eating bear [which really happens]. That momentary fact slip keeps the listeners from noticing the frozen lake, a cousin of upstate New York, New England, and Native American tales about races from summer into winter. And that reminds Harvey of a joke. . . .

By this time the one-on-one conversations and lie

45

swaps will have stopped. People will have quietly wandered in from the glove rack and the snack shelves. Harvey is still absorbed with one listener, delighted simply with the act of telling. He makes a passing reference to guiding and to city hunters, inverting the equation by casting himself as the greenhorn. His "loss" of the hunters is a fantasy this audience understands. It isn't easy to need work from someone whose ignorance can kill. It certainly isn't easy to be responsible for such a person in the woods. What relief to dispatch money, hunters, and guiding in one grand stroke of incompetence!

Harvey is warmed up. He plays with the actuality of getting lost in the woods, hooking us with details. We don't notice the transition until the momentum has carried us to the dream illogic of the lost simpleton who plays solitare to lure a kibitzer out of the forest. In a pace almost too quick to follow, the energy explodes in the old lucky accident sketch. The hunting image leads through a pun to another episode of the noodle bullied by an able animal.

The fishing stories remind Harvey of the rain in the living room and the brook trout in the driveway. And that makes him think of the earthquake, which leads him to the deep snow in winter and the September cold too extreme for a flatlander. It is an orgy of brilliant patterns of association and understated bragging. This is as close to collective self-congratulation as these folks come.

DROVE LOGS
DOWN STREAM

I done quite a lot of work up in this country, logging, lumberjacking, guiding, a little bit of everything. I did quite a lot of logging there for a while and we had that one summer where I cut seven thousand cord of pulp wood. What we did was we made a deal with the timber company, settled on a price and decided to cut the logs and drive them down the river.

So, we drove them down to Rock River and then into the Indian River and then into the Hudson River and we drove them all the way down, floated then all the way down to the paper mill. About 65 miles down there. When we got them down there, the guy down at the paper mill, the president or whoever he was, he came out and said, "Sorry boys, paper business isn't all that good now and we're going to have to cut the price a little bit."

I said. "How much you going to cut it?"

He said, "We're going to have to cut it three dollars a cord."

Well, that was quite a lot of money, so we said, "No way, no way at all. You're not going to get away with that."

And we drove those logs right back up the river again.

MUD SEASON

One spring, mud season they call it up here, the roads got so muddy that you could hardly get over them. It was too muddy to do any logging but I happened to have a big old horse there. It was back in the days of Model T's and the lights weren't too good on them, so they just drove mostly in the daytime.

Well, there was one big mud hole near the house here and I had a deal there. I'd wait down there with a horse and I'd pull those Model T's or the other old cars there when they got stuck. I'd tow them through the mud holes and make about so much money on them.

That worked out pretty good until it started to dry up. All the other mud holes in the country dried up except that one and I was still making pretty good money on towing cars through that mud hole. Then one night they caught me hauling water in to that mud hole and that was the end of that.

TAKE SPARKY
SNOW SHOEING

Ol' Sparky's kicking up a storm here. She's howling, and grumping and whining. She wants to take a trip to Rock Pond. I go back there about every day during the winter. I go back on snow shoes. I don't know if you know what snow shoes are, but they're kind of like an odd-shaped tennis racket. But I've got to get on my snow shoes and take Ol' Sparky for a walk back in the woods, I'll be right back.

I'm back. We had a good trip to Rock Pond; the snow was good and snow shoeing was nice and Sparky enjoyed it and I did too. And speaking of snow shoes, you know, back in the old days there we didn't have much money and we kind of liked to play tennis. But we didn't have any tennis balls or any tennis racket. So, what we had to do, we had to use a snow shoe and snow balls. That worked out pretty good until spring and then that was the end of that.

Used to do a lot of snow shoeing back in those days. There wasn't much else to do. We lived way back in the country then and kitty-corner across from another road there was the cutest little gal I ever saw. I used to like to go over and see her, but the problem was I weighed about 145 pounds and she had another fella who kind of liked her and he weighed about 180 pounds. So I didn't dare walk right up to the front door. What I'd do, I'd go to my back door and put on my snow shoes — this was the middle of the winter — and I'd go over on snow shoes to her back door and we'd go into the kitchen. We had a pretty good time, maybe a little apple cider, some popcorn or something and then I'd go back home. That went on pretty good all winter there. Then on in the spring, oh, it must have been pretty near the first of June, the snow was all gone and I looked up back of the house up in the edge of the woods and I could see something white. So, I went up and took a look at it. Well, what it was, was my snow shoe trail. It was about two feet wide and was about four feet high. I had made so many trips I had packed that snow right down tight. I still had a good trail there till the first of June. But the problem was that I figured if that other big boyfriend of hers ever saw that, he'd tear me to pieces. So that's when I left Tug Hill and moved to the Adirondacks.

REAL BEARS AND NOT REAL BEARS

We got a lot of snow there in Tug Hill and we got a lot of it in the Adirondacks too. Actually, you don't even call it good snow until it ages for a couple of years and then it gets pretty good. It gets kind of scarce in the summer but what's left is pretty good snow.

We get a lot of snow, a lot of winter out there, a lot of cold weather. Here up till two or three years ago the phone booth outdoors across the post office got so cold you couldn't get the dial to work. So they put a heater in the phone booth and that made it pretty nice. You'd get in there and you could make your phone calls and you wouldn't freeze to death. That worked pretty good for a while, but then they had to take the doggone heater out of the phone booth. What happened was the bears discovered that phone booth was heated and every bear in the neighborhood wanted to hibernate in there. Well, they had an awful hassle and they almost tore that phone booth apart.

There are quite a lot of bears up here. You see more of them during the summer. Turn around and go up the dumps at Long Lake or Indian Lake and you can see quite a few bear

51

up there. Of course, the one thing that I've got to tell you about that, is that not all of them are real bears. A lot of them are just unemployed lumberjacks.

The logging isn't too good up in this country and there isn't much work for the lumberjacks, so what they do, they hire these lumberjacks. They give them a fur coat and a fur parka and some black mittens and boots and they take them up to the dumps and they tear around, put on a show and they do a pretty good job of it. But what you've got to do, you got to get up there before midnight because they got their own little union and after midnight they charge time and a half for being bears and the town can't afford to pay that.

I got to tell you about a little experience I had here a year or so ago with a black bear. I was up picking blackberries and of course the black bear, they like blackberries too. I had one pail just about full and I set that down and started picking in the other pail. I looked over and that old bear had his head right in my pail and boy, he was chomping those berries right down as fast as he could. Well, about that time I got a little bit peeved. So, I came right up behind him and I kicked him one. Well, then he got peeved and he started after me. I weighed about 160 pounds and he must have weighed about 400. We ran, and we ran, and we ran and I just couldn't get away from him. I could stay ahead of him but I couldn't get away from him and I stayed just ahead of him there, oh, for quite a while. Finally we got down to Blue Mountain Lake. I got out on the ice and the ice was so slippery, the old bear couldn't stand up on it and then I got away from him. You might kind of wonder about blackberry season and walking on the ice, but that was a long race. He chased me right through the middle of December and we had about a foot of ice by that time.

I have found out since then how you keep a bear from charging. All you got to do is take away his credit card.

GUIDING IN THE
ADIRONDACKS

There's a lot of different ways of making a living up here and I've tried most of them. I used to do quite a little guiding. I was out one day with a fella, a guy from down in the city. I took him out and it got snowing and blowing pretty good and it was pretty hard to see and I got a little bit mixed up myself. And he looked at me and said, "What's the matter, are you lost?"

"No, I'm not lost. I'm a little bit confused, I ain't lost."

"Well," he said, "I thought you told me you're the best guide in the Adirondacks?"

I said, "Well, I think I am, but I'm afraid you're in the Catskills now!"

Another day I took two fellas out. Times were hard and money was scarce, but they were going to give me two dollars a piece to guide them that day. Well, I went out with them and I lost two hunters and four dollars and that was the end of my guiding.

I was kind of a greenhorn woodsman myself when I started hunting and I was a little bit worried about getting lost. I asked this old-timer there who knew the woods like a book and he said, "Well, nothing to worry about, if

you get lost all you have to do is shoot the signal."

I asked him, "What's the signal?"

"Well," he said, "the best signal is a long pause and one quick shot."

So I got lost and I took a long pause and one quick shot and then I listened. Then nothing happened and pretty soon I shot again and I listening. Nothing happened, nobody ever did come to find me. Finally I stumbled through the woods and I found my way out and I decided that was the end of my bow and arrow hunting.

Later on I learned that one thing that can come in handy and doesn't take up much room is a deck of cards. Then if you should get lost, you just find a big old stump or a flat rock or something and you start playing solitaire. Boy, it won't be five minutes some joker'll come along and say, "Hey, put that black jack on the red queen." Then you can ask him how to get out of the woods.

Well, then I took up black powder muzzle loading hunting and I thought that was a pretty good idea. You just loaded up yourself, you didn't have to buy shells and all that stuff. So, I went up one day, right in the middle of deer season. I got to the edge of the woods and well, I decided to load the old rifle right up. So I loaded up the old muzzle loader and then I pulled out my pipe and I filled that up. I wasn't going to smoke it then but I said, "A little later

I'll want to smoke it." So, I filled it up and put it in my pocket and I went on hunting.

As I got up in the woods, and I was tippy toeing along — boy, I saw a nice buck there. A beautiful buck with a nice rack which could hold about 15 hats, I guess. I pulled right up dead center on him with the old muzzle loader and I pulled the trigger and all there was was just a little click. Well, that was kind of funny, so I pulled right up again. Maybe I didn't pull the trigger hard enough, so I pulled the trigger again and got another click. Well, I couldn't see any future in that. The old rifle wasn't going to work, so I set it down and leaned it up against a tree and pulled out my old pipe to light it up and think it over and maybe check the rifle out a little bit.

I put the old pipe in my mouth and I lit it and boy, it made the biggest BOOM! you ever heard in your life. It made an awful racket. I guess what I did was I got my black powder and my tobacco mixed up. It blew that old pipe all to pieces and blew all the hair off my head and it never did grow back again and so I've been a little more careful with a muzzle loader since then.

DUCKS

I did all kinds of hunting up here, rabbits and birds, deer, bear and buffalo, whatever I could find up here. But one day I was duck hunting down on Lake Durant and got off into the tag alders there and the cattails and got my boat all set up and put my decoys out and had my old dog, Get'um, with me. I called him "Get'um" because he was a great little retriever. I'd just holler "get'um" and he would go get them.

Well, we sat there waiting. It got a little chilly but here comes a flock of ducks and I pulled up and shot. The old gun kicked pretty good and I kind of blinked my eyes and looked and I guess I didn't get one because the dog never moved. Ole Get'um sat right there in the boat. So here came some more ducks and oh, I shot again and looked and the old dog just sat there. Well, I kept trying anyway. The ducks, they were flying like crazy. They fly pretty fast. In fact, a doctor put me on a diet and wouldn't let me eat ducks because he didn't want me eating that fast food. Well, anyhow, we sat there and pretty soon another flock of ducks went over and I shot again and son of a gun, Ole Get'um jumped right out of the boat and away he went and back he came with a

duck and put it in the boat. Away he went and back he came with another duck. Well, I didn't think I got two ducks in one shot. But away he went again and back he came with another duck. Then I looked a little bit closer and those were my decoys. I had a dozen decoys out there. Ole Get'um, he picked up all twelve of the decoys, dumped them in the boat and then hopped in and sat there in the back seat. I had to take them home. He didn't like the way I hunted ducks.

Speaking of ducks, we had quite a rain here a while ago. When it was over it was kind of peaceful-like the way them ducks were swimming around. There were some big ducks and some little ducks, all just swimming around real peaceful-like. The only problem was that was in my living room. Like I said, it rained pretty hard that day.

After that rain, I got a nice mess of brook trout — right out in my drive way. One of them was, oh, about a six-inch trout I guess. Of course, that's measuring between the eyes.

EARTHQUAKES AND OTHER WEATHER

We have all kinds of weather up here, quite a lot of rain, quite a lot of snow sometimes. We even had a little earthquake here a few years ago. It didn't amount to too much, about 5.3 on the Richter Scale, and there wasn't much damage. Just one chimney fell over here in town, but they claimed the guy that owned the chimney was kind of pushing at it at the time. Nobody really got hurt. One lady, though, she wasn't feeling well for a while after that earthquake. She was sleeping on a water bed and she was sea sick for about a week.

We have all kinds of weather up here. Got a lot of snow last winter. It powdered out, but the roads got so narrow the dogs had to wag their tails up and down and if you went down the middle of the road in a snowmobile you'd skin both elbows.

Last fall about this time of the year, a little after Labor Day, a fella was working up here who'd been here all summer. Then it got a little bit colder — dropped down to about 40 degrees. He shook himself a little bit and he said, "I'm getting kind of chilly, I think I better go get my jacket."

And I said "Where's your jacket?"

He said, "In Tucson, Arizona."

I guess the summer's over now. They closed the beach again. They didn't have it opened long this year. They got a town ordinance about the beach there. They don't open the beach in the spring until after the ice goes out. I think they opened it on a Thursday and closed it on the weekend.

When I was fourteen, Dad taught me to pull cross-cut saw with him," Harvey remembers. As an older teenager, Harvey began to work in the woods on his own. He went back to the same boss every year. He was a peeler first. Later, he stabled and took care of the teamsters' horses. One spring, when there was no cook in camp, the lumberjacks talked Harvey into cooking. A "guy at the hotel in Athens used beer in his pancake batter. He said it made them light." From somewhere in his marvelous memory bank came the old tale about the flying pancake, to mix with the beer in the batter, to make the story.

These tellings at the corner store are low-keyed exchanges among long-time neighbors. In a sense, the main character of every story is the Adirondack wilderness. The fish eager to be caught, the joke-lie about the confusion of the photograph with the original, the contests and lying retorts between woodsman and warden are elements of their common, regional repertoire. The raccoon Harvey wanted to trap is related to squirrels told about in other parts of the United States who run five feet into the air before they realize their favorite tree has been cut down. The comment that he ". . . didn't want the trees cut down, and . . . didn't want to hurt the coon," is an indicator of values he shares with the men around the table.

Harvey likes to cast himself as the bonehead, as he did one time when my call interrupted checkbook balancing. "There's never any problem. I get the bank's final figure and my final figure. If they don't agree, I just put down, 'ESP-error someplace!' It works every time!"

64

The comic hero is the master of disguise. It is as if we have witnessed a sleight-of hand performance in which just the right image threads through the best procession of tales, paced with the most apt jokes, told with the straightest face and the most modest manner.

PANCAKES

I'll have to tell you about a little experience up in hunting camp. I like to get up early in the morning anyway and a lot of the boys like to sleep in, so they sort of elected me as the cook for breakfast. Well, that was O.K. They'd carry in the wood and they'd do the dishes. So that worked out pretty good.

We had a big, old fireplace there and a big grill right in the middle of it. I was going to make some pancakes, so I looked at the recipe and then somebody mentioned that if you put some beer in the pancake batter, it'll make the pancakes come out lighter. I dumped in some beer and made a few pancakes and, sure enough, they were lighter, puffed right up nice. So the next time around I put in some more beer and they came up lighter yet.

"Well," I said "if a little bit is good, lots is better."

So I dumped in a whole bunch of beer the last trip there and that's the only liquid I put in.

Well, those pancakes got so light they puffed up and they wouldn't even stay on the grill. They would come up off of the grill and start right up the chimney. I had to go out and get a bunch of little flat rocks and I put a little flat

rock on top of each pancake. That worked pretty good until the rocks got so hot I couldn't handle them and I couldn't do that anymore. Then the pancakes started to go right up the chimney. I had to put the ladder up and put a guy up there with a landing net to catch the pancakes as they came out of the chimney. Then he'd bring them back down. They weren't too bad, a little bit cool but they tasted pretty good yet.

Well, that worked pretty good until one of the boys, he had a shotgun there, got out there with his shotgun and was trap shooting my pancakes. It actually didn't hurt the taste too much. It did poke them full of holes, but we ate them and they tasted good. It was a little bit aggravating, though, to spit the birdshot out of those pancakes.

RACCOONS

One day I was hunting up there all alone. I wish somebody had been with me so they could have seen it too. I looked and there came a raccoon out of the top of a tree. He slipped down the outside of the tree and he went back in through a hole in the bottom. I looked up and here he came, out the top of the tree again. Then, just like before, he slid down the outside and went in the bottom again. I kept looking and here he came out of the top of the tree again, slid down the outside and went in the bottom.

Well, that was kind of curious but I had some hunting to do. So I went on. But when I got back in to the camp I kept thinking about that raccoon. So the next morning I took the saw back in there and I cut that hollow tree down to see what the story was. And what it turned out to be was a tree full of coons with one coon left over. And everytime one went in at the bottom it pushed another one out the top.

I was out there another day and I looked up at this little tree there. It was about 40 feet high, I guess, and kind of slim. I looked up and here was a bobcat right up in the top of it. Well, I thought I was going to have some fun so

I decided to shimmy up the tree and shake that bobcat. So, I shimmied up the tree and the closer I got, the bobcat kept getting up further and further. He got way up on the limber little top of the tree and I shook and I shook and, sure enough, I shook him out of there. Down he come!

I was about to start back down when I looked and here comes the bobcat back up again right behind me! Well, the closer he got the further up I went. Then he started shaking the tree. Well, he shook and shook and finally I had to let go and down I came and it knocked the wind right out of me. Well, I was a little peeved and I said, "He can't get away with that!"

So up the tree I went up again and I shook him out of there and down he came. Well, he was kind of mad too, I guess. He came right back up the tree again and chased me way out on a skinny little branch there and shook and shook and down I came!

Well, that was enough of that. I grabbed my rifle and I went back to deer hunting.

I was out there another day hiking through the woods and I see this little raccoon. He was a cute little fellow, about half grown and if you catch them young enough you can tame them. They're pretty friendly until they start getting old and then they get mean. So, I took a run for him. I got pretty near to him and boy, away he went, up this slim little tree there, oh, 30 feet

high I guess, and probably six to eight inches through. Away he went right up that tree.

Well, I was on state land there and I didn't want to cut the tree and I didn't want to hurt the coon, so I went on my way. By golly, though, I came back the next day and I caught him on the ground again! He was picking up beechnuts, I guess. They were pretty thick right there. I tried to catch him and up that same tree he went again. Well, it happened about six days in a row. I never could quite catch up with him. He would get up that tree before I could get to him.

So finally I went one day there and I looked and he was nowhere in sight. He was off over the hill somewhere. Well, I cut that tree off at the height of about six or seven feet and then I took off. Next day I came back and there's that little coon, he's on the ground again picking up beechnuts, so I took after him and he headed for that tree. Of course the whole top of the tree was gone. Well, he got up there to where I cut it off and he kept right on going. I had my landing net there, the one I usually use for brook trout fishing. After he'd gone up about twenty feet beyond the top of that tree stub he realized there wasn't no tree there anymore and he started to fall. When he came down I stuck out my landing net and I caught him and I had myself a coon.

PARTRIDGE
ONE AT A TIME

I took my old dog Sparky partridge hunting one day. She wasn't really a bird dog but she'd rattle around and sometimes she'd find a partridge for me. I went out with her one day and took my buddy Joe along. We got up in the woods and all of a sudden I looked and, boy, Ol' Sparky, she was froze right there. There was partridge up there. Away she went. I couldn't see what was going on but I pretty much knew what she was up too.

So I waited a bit and then said, "O.K., Sparky"

Up come a partridge. I shot and I got it.

I said, "O.K." and there came another partridge and I got that.

"You get the next one, Joe," I said.

So I hollered "O.K." and he shot at the next one. Well, he was getting excited by that time and he missed and I said, "O.K." again and here come another one and I got it. And that was about it. We had enough partridge.

Joe said, "What in the world is going on around here? Ol' Sparky's out there and those partridges are coming up like that one at a time just when you holler."

I said, "Well, I tell you what she does. She

chases them all into a hollow log and puts her paw over the hole and then she lets them out one at a time when I'm ready for them."

BLACK FLIES
ON THE HOOK

I'll tell you a little more about some of my fishing trips and some of the fun I had. It's quite a sport, fishing. I fish a little of everything, fly fishing and everything else. I like fly fishing but the trouble is when the black flies are biting that's the type of lure you're supposed to use. That's the kind of fly you're supposed to use to catch brook trout. Then it's hard. Those little buggers are so small and squirmy, it's hard to tie them on a hook, but after you get one on, you'll probably catch a fish.

I got one secret stream up there. One stream where I always have good luck. It's kind of a secret, I don't tell people about it. It's a real good place to catch brook trout. The one thing you have to look out for is you have to hide behind a tree to bait your hook or the fish will come right out and grab it.

That's my secret fishing place. I was up there one day and boy, they were really biting. I got one. I got a big one. I don't know how much it weighed. I didn't have any scales there, and I was way back in the woods and it was pretty warm weather and I had to eat it. So, I never did find how much it weighed, but I had my little Brownie camera there and I took a picture of it and when I got that picture developed, that little snapshot weighed 11 pounds.

These fisherman, they always have their own way of doing things. Their own secret ways of catching trout or fish of any kind. Some fisherman stand there and fish and some fisherman sit there and fish, and some fisherman just lie.

6 TROUT AND
12 TROUT = 18

I try to be a good law-abiding citizen and so I go and follow the game laws. Once
in a while I get carried away a little bit, but not
too bad. I went out there one day, oh, about a
year ago. The water was kind of high and I
went out fishing, and I fished and I fished and
I tried hard and I got six brook trout. Well, the
limit was ten, so I went home with my six
brook trout anyhow and I went back and I
waited a couple of days and the water went
down. And I went back again and the water
had gone down and fishing was pretty good
and I got twelve. I said, "Well that's enough of
that." So I started for home. Well, I met the
game warden.

He said, "How's the fishing?"

And I said "Pretty good, I caught twelve."

He said, "Twelve?"

I said, "Sure."

So I showed them to him and he said, "I'm
the game warden You're only supposed to catch
10 fish a day. I'm going to give you a ticket for
that."

I said, "Now look, I was here a couple of
days ago and I fished real hard and only got six
trout and I come back today and I caught

78

twelve trout. So six and twelve are eighteen. I think you owe me two fish."

He said, "You get yourself two more fish and get the hell out of here."

FISHING WITH
A CARROT

Another time I was out fishing on private land. It's a real nice pond there and big signs all over the place say "No Fishing," but I sat there and I was fishing away and I see the game warden coming so I got ready for him.

The game warden comes and he says "Hey, you're not supposed to fish here."

And I said, "No?"

He said, "See that sign? It says, 'No Fishing.' "

I said, "Well, all I'm using is a carrot." and I pulled it out and sure enough I had a carrot on my hook.

And he took one look at it and he looked at me kind of funny like and, "Well, O.K., I guess," he said and away he went. Well, he came back about a half an hour later. Geez, I had five or six nice brook trout laying there on the bank.

He said, "Now, don't tell me that you caught those trout on the carrot."

I said, "No, I caught you on that one."

STEELHEAD TROUT

I got to tell you how we catch steelhead trout up here. What you got to do here on Blue Mountain Lake, you got to wait till the late fall, early winter, wait till you get about three inches of good blue ice, enough ice to hold you. Then you go out and what you do, is you just put your favorite lure on there, a minnow or a spinner or a worm or some artificial lure of some sort. And what you do is you take your pole and line up and you lay that lure on the ice and you walk kind of fast-like right across that ice and them old steelhead trout if they're hitting they'll come right up through that ice and they'll nail that lure, or whatever you have on there. And then you've got yourself a nice fish there.

I guess that's one reason they call them steelheads.

Grampa holds court in the back room: putting down the gullible tourist, parodying the hero's sacrifice. The pendulum with the sharp shadow is an example of a tall tale conceit, *or the absurd disregard for the nature of a material object. (See Carolyn S. Brown*, The Tall Tale in American Folklore and Literature, *Knoxville, University of Tennessee Press, 1987.) Clocks with unusual shadows have also been found in Pennsylvania and Indiana. "Cold River Beaver" looks in on daily life in the logging bunkhouse, foiled by that ultimate survivor, the beaver. The assigning of human traits to animals is an example of the* category mistake, *the creation of ". . . an absurdity by allocating an object or concept to a logical type or category to which it does not belong." (Gilbert S. Ryle in Brown*, The Tall Tale *. . .). The meeting of the turkey hunters is one of the few examples in Harvey's work of that stock device known in comic drama as* doubling. *The other example provides the title for this collection.*

"Parachute Gas Stove" suggests the violence without consequence of the roadrunner cartoons. Harvey recalls this joke from his stint as a paratrooper in World War II. He ". . . remodeled it to fit the Adirondacks."

83

A LITTLE BIT
ABOUT GRAMPA

I should tell you a little bit about my old Grampa. He is quite a boy. He is one of the old-timers. He is rough and he was tough, but he's pretty cool and collected. He never got too excited. One night there Ma said, "Harvey, go up and tell Grampa to come for supper." So, I went out and I looked and looked and I went up way up and who was up in the woods there, way up in the woods and there stood Grampa.

I said, "Grampa, supper's ready."

He just stood there and he said, "Yep."

And I said, "Ain't you coming to supper?"

He said, "Nope."

And I said, "Grampa, why not?"

"Well", he said, "I can't."

And I said. "Why can't you?".

"Well," he said, "I'm standing in a bear trap."

Nope, he never got too excited about things.

Back in his days there, they used to catch bears alive and they'd put them in cages and keep them. Grampa used to go out and he'd catch these cub bears and some a little bigger than a cub. He would catch them and he'd wrestle them and tie their feet together. He'd keep them for a while and then sell them to a zoo or something. One day he was up there in the back lot and I heard kind of a fracas. So I ran up there to see what was going on and there's old Grampa. He had a bear there that was bigger than a cub, more like a yearling. Boy, they were in the middle of an awful hassle. Grampa, he was trying to do something with that bear. They were going around and around and around.

I looked at him and I hollered, "Hey Grampa, you want me to help hold that bear?"

"No," he said, "I don't need that but I wouldn't mind a bit if you'd help me let go of him."

That Grampa of mine, he was a great old boy. He really belonged up in the Adirondacks here. He really liked it. He sat at the station there one morning having a cup of coffee and somebody walked up and said, "Hi there, old timer, have you lived here all your life?"

And Grampa said, "No, not yet."

And then the guy looked up at the wall and there's a sign says "50 Cents a Cup," and he said, "Holy Mackerel, that's a lot of money for a cup of coffee. I remember when you could buy a cup of coffee for a nickel."

Grampa looked at the sign and looked at this guy and said, "Yep, I remember them times and I didn't have the nickel."

The guy said, "Maybe you're right about

that. Hey, do you know of any good places to fish?"

And Grampa said, "Well, you go right out here to Blue Mountain Lake and you go over to West Bay and you find a good level spot and you fish right there."

We got Grampa's picture hanging up there over the mantle and then there is another picture frame there and right in the middle of that frame all there is is a sliver, oh, about the size of a lead pencil, I guess. Well, what it is, it's from way back in hard times there, when we didn't have much money and an awful cold winter we didn't have much wood. Well, poor old Grampa had lost a leg and he had a wooden leg. It kept getting colder and colder and the wood pile ran out and finally we looked at Grampa and looked at that wooden leg. Finally Grampa said, "Well, go ahead use it, put it in the fire. We don't want to freeze to death."

We used his wooden leg but we did take a sliver out of it and put it in that picture frame and that's up on the wall. If you look close you'll see an inscription there, "A sliver from my Grampa's wooden leg."

Quite a guy, Ole Grampa. He used to have a grandfather clock there. Well, now he passed away, but we still got the clock and you know that that clock is so old that just the shadow of the pendulum going back and forth has worn a hole through the back of the clock.

HARD TIMES

Things are pretty good right now. Times are pretty good and we get along pretty well, but it wasn't always that way. It used to be way back during the Depression times everybody got skinny. Even the piggy bank would get skinny. You know people holler now because they don't have color television if it's in the shop or something. Well, when I was a young lad during the Depression all we had was black and white crayons.

We got along pretty good, though. One winter there, things got pretty rough and my buddy and I decided to go to a town, oh, 30 miles away where nobody knew us and see if we could pick up a square meal or two. So we went down there. It was quite a hike. We got down there after a while and we walked up to a nice house, there and walked up and knocked on the door and a lady answered the door and said, "Can I help you?"

So, I showed her this little card and on the card it said "I am deaf and dumb and I have had nothing to eat today and I am very hungry."

She read the card and she looked at my buddy and said, "Oh, are you deaf and dumb too?"

And he said "Yes Ma'am, I sure am."

Boy, she put the run on both of us!

We went to another house down the road a ways and went up and knocked on the door and I decided not to play deaf and dumb, so I just said, "Lady, we're awful hungry. We didn't have a thing to eat all day and wonder if you can spare us a bite?"

So she said "You see that pile of wood over there."

So I looked over and there is this big pile of wood and a buck saw and a saw horse. And I looked at my buddy and he didn't look very happy about it either and I said "What did you say Ma'am?"

She said "Did you see that wood over there?"

And I said "No, I didn't."

She said "Well, I saw you see it."

"Well," I said, "Maybe you saw me see it but you're not going to see me saw it."

You know we didn't get anything to eat at that house either.

COLD RIVER BEAVER

Things used to be pretty rough up here, but not as rough as it was up in Cold River. I spent the winter up there one year and that was cold. I mean cold up there. Now, we had a little trouble. We had our bunkhouse and we had a water line run from there down into the river. It was all nice pure water there anyway and we had this line pumped up in one of them old cistern pumps up in the bunkhouse. Yeah, we'd pump it and pump it and get whatever water we would need to wash up with. That worked pretty good for a while. Then all of a sudden, one day, we pumped and pumped and nothing happened. It was pretty cold that morning. So we decided to try something. We had some hot water there and we poured hot water down through the pipe and pumped and boy, away it went. Then it worked good.

The next morning the same thing happened and we just poured some hot water down through the pipe there and it worked alright again. Well, we had to thaw that out about every morning for a while. Then we had a warm spell there. It warmed right up and was warm and rainy there for a couple of days. Well, we got up in the morning and started pumping and no water would come. We all said it must be froze up again. So we poured some hot water down through there and just as we were pouring it in there I happened to think.

I said, "Now wait a minute. It s been thawing here for two or three days, how could that pipe freeze up?"

"That's right," they said.

I said, "You just wait till I get down there and when I holler you dump that hot water in there."

So down I went. I got right down to the river and I hollered "O.K.!" and they dumped that hot water in there. That's when I saw what it was. It was an old beaver. It would come along with that old flat tail of his, put it right over the end of the pipe and block it up so we'd think it was froze up and would pour that hot water down in there. Then that old beaver would move his tail, take a shower in the hot water and away he'd go.

TURKEY

We had our turkey season up here. A couple or three years ago and I decided to go out and see if I could get myself a turkey. They're a pretty wise animal and especially those old toms there. Boy, they can run like a deer and hide almost anywhere and they're pretty tricky.

What you've got to do, you've got to get a turkey call and you blow on it kinda like a duck call or something but it sounds more like a turkey. You take that and you blow the turkey call on it and you sit there and listen and try to draw one up to you. So, I went out one day and I sat down and found a good place there and I got pretty well out of sight and I blew on my turkey call, a couple or three times. All of a sudden I got an answer. Well, that sounded good, but he was quite aways away. So I blew on my call again and he answered a little bit closer and I said, "I better sit right here and let him do the moving towards me."

So, I'd blow and everytime he'd answer me he'd be a little closer. Finally it got up pretty close. And I said, "Boy that's within shooting distance now. I think I can get a shot at it and get myself a turkey." So I threw the old gun up and I jumped right up quick and aimed . . . but there stood another turkey hunter with another turkey call. So, I didn't get my turkey.

PARACHUTE GAS STOVE

I spend most of my time here in the Adirondacks, or up in the hills somewhere. I think I was born up in the hills under a hemlock tree or something. But during WW II I was in the 101st Airborne Division and I was a paratrooper. That worked out pretty good. I never even got a scratch during the war. When I came out, we had a camp way up, that was in Cold River. Had a camp way up here, about an 18 mile hike to get in there. Well, I had an idea there. The other guys were going to hike in. So, I said, "I'll give you a day to get in there and you get in there and get the fires going and so on, and tomorrow I will have a fella bring me over there in an airplane and I'll jump and bail out and see if I can come down right by camp."

They said "O.K." and set out hiking early one morning and I waited till the next morning and the sun came up good and I got in the airplane and I said, "O.K.," take me up over Cold River till I can see that tent and I'll see how close I can come to it."

So he took me over there and I got right over the tent and I jumped. Well, you know that main parachute did not open, but I had an emergency chute on there and I pulled the string on that and that didn't open. By that time I was going down pretty fast, when what should I see but one of my buddies coming up. I hollered at him as he went past, "Hey Joe, do you know anything about parachutes?"

He hollered back at me, "No, do you know anything about lighting a gas stove?"

Carr is a prime example of what Richard Dorson calls a sagaman, *a yarnspinner who makes himself the hero of localized migratory motifs. (Richard Dorson,* Bloodstoppers and Bearwalkers, *Cambridge, Harvard University Press, 1952.) "Garden Tops and Bottoms" resets a widespread old anecdote about the division of crops between a foolish and a clever partner. Growing rock claims are found in Wales, Hereford, the English Midlands, Canada, and the hill farm territory east of the Mississippi.*

A commonplace at rural diners and bars and gas stations in the Adirondacks is that representatives of the law, the school, and the government don't have much sense. In "Lawn, Wetlands, and Wilderness" the scorn extends to environmentalists.

Woodsmen's carnivals, or field days, are traditional contests of work skills. Like rodeos and firemen's field days, they are competitive games designed to maintain skills necessary for dangerous occupations. Harvey uses the setting for a numskull's invention and a reverse brag.

LAWN, WETLANDS AND WILDERNESS

I had a little hassle with the APA here a while ago. It was back here about May when we had that real rainy spell and there was water everywhere, enough so ducks were swimming around in my living room.

It got pretty wet and the grass started growing and it was getting pretty high. So, I went out and I was going to mow the lawn when this guy stopped. He pulled over and he said, "I'm with the APA and I'm checking up on you people. You can't mow that lawn."

And I said. "Why can't I?"

"Well," he said, "we've got that classified as a wetland."

So I took the mower and I put it away. Well, then the grass in my lawn got higher and the weeds started to grow and the brush started growing up there and I said to myself the least I can do is cut that brush out of there. I got the old axe and I was going to chop that brush and get that out of there when here came that same guy from the APA.

"Look," he said, "you can't cut that brush. We reclassified it and now that's a wilderness area."

SHINGLING

We got all kind of different weather up here. It gets pretty foggy sometimes. Once in a while it gets so foggy they have to plow the roads to get the fog off it. You can't get through it with a car.

During one of those fogs we were shingling a roof. We started at the bottom like you always do and we were tacking those shingles on and it was pretty foggy. We kept tacking them on, tacking them on and kept going up and up and up. It seemed to be taking an awful long time. Then one of the guys with me took a closer looked and he yelled, "Hey we're over top the roof. We're just shingling out on the fog."

So we stopped and then I said, "Wait a minute, let's see if we can use that to some advantage."

So what we did, we measured the roof from the eaves on the side we were on and measured from the eaves right up to the peak. Well then we measured right up onto the fog there the same distance — about 20 feet further. Then we tacked right on top of that fog. Well, when the fog dissipated the shingles settled right down onto the roof and it fit just like a glove.

HOW I INVENTED THE CHAIN SAW

I used to have quite a little time with the chain saw there. I've used chain saws quite a lot. In fact, I invented the chain saw. Made the first saw that was ever made. What I did was I just took an old bucksaw and I took a hunk of that furnace chain and I put there right in there and I tightened that up pretty good and boy, it made a good 'un. It was quiet, and light and easy to carry. It didn't cut all that great, but then they started putting motors on them and that was the end of my chain saw.

I got used to that motorized chain saw after that. In fact, one trip I went down to Booneville to the Woodsman's Field Day and I got into a chain saw race. What they do, they blow a whistle and then you start cutting and they wait two minutes and they blow another whistle they see how much wood you'd have cut. I entered the race and when I got done and they started measuring up and I had a cord and a half of wood. The guy right next to me, though, had just a little bit more. He had a cord and 5/8's, maybe. I felt pretty bad about that, because I thought my chain saw was right in top shape and everything. So, that bothered me quite a bit. Well, I got home and I was pacing back and forth and feeling pretty bad about it.

My wife, Mary, said, "That's funny, you've always been pretty good with a chain saw." So, she went out and looked and she came back in and said "Well, Harve, no wonder you didn't win first prize. You had your chain on backwards."

Then I put the chain on right, and I touched it up, just so. It was a whisker sharper I guess. Then I went out in the back yard. I had a wood pile there. I said, "I guess I'll try it now and cut for just about two minutes."

You know, in two minutes, I had two truck loads of sawdust.

GARDEN TOPS AND BOTTOMS

Well, I got to tell you a little more about my garden up here. I have a pretty good garden usually. The ground is a little hard there in spots. In fact, the cornfield area you have to plant with a shotgun. But when it grows, it grows pretty good. I used to have a partner. We went in partners there for a couple of years. We shared all the expenses and did about the same amount of work and we made an agreement before we planted the garden.

My buddy said "Well, what do you say, you take the tops and I'll take the bottoms?"

I said, "O.K., that sounds good."

So I took the tops and he took the bottoms and then I said, "What are we going to plant this year?"

He said, "What do you say we plant carrots?"

So we planted carrots. Well, needless to say, I didn't make out very good that year. The next year we decided to go in partnership again. But I said to myself, "I got to be a little more careful this time." I got to keep my eye on this guy. He's a little bit sharp. So we made the agreement we would share the expenses and save an amount of money for the seeds and fertilizer and do the same amount of work.

I said, "Only one thing, this year I want the bottoms."

He said, "Yeah, that's OK."

Then I said, "Well, what are we going to plant?"

"Well," he said "We're going to plant cabbages."

I didn't turn out very good that year either, so that broke up our partnership.

ROCK GARDEN
GROWING GOOD

Speaking of gardens, I have to tell you a little bit about my rock garden. That's coming along good. About a year ago I only planted one rock, oh, about the size of a football, I guess, when I planted it, and that did pretty well. That grew up to about the size of a washtub now. I did so well, I got some more small rocks and I'm going to plant them in the spring, just as soon as the frost goes out of the ground. It looks like I might have a pretty good rock garden there.

I think I'm going to be careful and not get them too close together, because the way that one grew, its going to take a lot of room.

I have another kind of a special rock there, but I'm going to save that one. I don't think I better plant that. That's my pet rock. Almost everybody has a pet rock, but this one is kind of unusual. Don't ask me how come, but it floats.

What happened was I was down in Lake Ontario, surf-dipping for smelt. I looked and I saw something white floating up onto the shore. I figured it was probably a Clorax bottle, but when I walked up and I looked here was this rock. It had floated up to shore. I picked it up and looked it over and it was pretty heavy. I said to myself it was kind of unusual to see a rock float out of the lake like that, so I kept it.

"Not Lies, But Experiences," Harvey's standard disclaimer, is followed by his musing about how nice it would be to have a bear's suit, feet and all, for snowmobiling! The joke about the tackle box hints that news about "equality" may not have reached Blue Mountain Lake, where everyone understands that wives are in charge. The great porcupine catch echoes the one about trapping a poltergeist, a noisy ghost, under a chamber pot. The silly problem of what to do when you catch something you don't want anyway goes back at least to DeFoe's Moll Flanders, standing in her garret with the horse she couldn't keep from stealing.

Travel accounts of the seventeenth and eighteenth centuries described marvelous creatures, including hoop snakes. No one but Harvey Carr, however, would make those hoop snakes into automobile tires — and put two on backwards. No one.

A parrot who bids himself up at the auction? Why not? Anything can happen when the simpleton goes to town.

NOT LIES, EXPERIENCES

I have done quite a lot of talking here, telling quite a few things that have happened up in this country. Of course, you know, I'm not really much of a story teller. I do belong to this Adirondack Liars Club along with Bill Smith, Joe Bruchac and a few other of the boys there. Those guys can tell some pretty good stories,. I wouldn't say they were lying but if it came to a serious case where they really had to lie, I'd think maybe they'd be up to it.

I really don't care much about lying and I don't tell tall stories, but I just wanted to remind you that these are unusual experiences that I happened to have had.

In fact, I'm not so sure I lie anyway. I have some unusual experiences and I tell some stories even though they may be true, but I don't believe I really lie. Looked it up in the dictionary one day and it said to "lie" l-i-e, is to deceive and to deceive is to tell somebody something even though it is not true and make them believe it. Then you're deceiving them and you're lying to them. Now I don't believe you folks are believing me anyway, so I don't think I am lying to you. I don't think I'm deceiving you and so I must be telling the truth.

105

165–170 POUND BEAR

Well, the early bear season started now, started last week I guess, and I don't go too much for hunting bear. I tried it once, and I got cold. After that I put my hunting clothes on and that was better.

What I'd really like to find is the right size bear. One thing I never did, I never got the bear I was after. I was after a bear there for, oh, several years and never get one the right size. I didn't want a great big one and I didn't want a little cub or anything. What I wanted, I wanted one that weighed about 170 pounds. Then all I'd have to do is skin him out and leave the legs and feet on. Put a zipper up the front and boy, I would have a snowmobile suit that wouldn't stop.

NOTE IN TACKLE BOX

Well, I'm feeling pretty good again now. For a while there I wasn't feeling all that great. I was kind of bumped and bruised and pretty well lamed up. What had happened is that my wife threw my fishing jacket out of the upstairs window. That wouldn't have been so bad except that I was in it at the time.

I really don't know what she was all that perturbed about. Maybe it was about that fishing trip I went on the week before. We got our equipment all together, and tackle and everything and went on our fishing trip. Well, we had a pretty good time, the boys and I. We were gone overnight. When I got back home and Mary says, "Well, how was the fishing?"

I said, "Well, not too good. I must have tried everything in that tackle box and they wouldn't hit on any of it."

She said, "Did you get my note?"

I said, "No, what note?"

She said, "The note I put right in the top of your tackle box."

I don't know, maybe that's what she was all perturbed about because that's when she threw my jacket out the window.

CATCH A PORCUPINE
WITH WASH TUB

You know, I used to like to catch wild animals when they were kind of young and make pets of them. I've had raccoons and flying squirrels and I kinda tamed quite a lot of animals. One animal I never did get to tame was a porcupine A guy said, "Well, they make a pretty good pet. You have to be kind of careful how you pet them, though."

So I said, "How do you catch one?"

"Well," he said, "You have to catch them on the ground and then you take a big old washtub and you run right out there. They're pretty slow, anyway. You run right up and you slap that washtub right on top of them and you got em."

I said, "What do you do next?"

"Well," he said, "You sit down on that washtub and figure out your next move."

HOOP SNAKES

We got some odd creatures up in this country and one of them is the hoop snake. I don't know if you ever saw a hoop snake or not, probably not. They are not poisonous but they're different from most snakes. They're not very plentiful, but we got them up here. The way they travel is to take their tail right in their mouth and they form themselves into a ring and then they roll wherever they're going to go and boy, then can they go pretty fast. Well, being kind of inventive, I got an idea. You know, I like to invent things. And in fact, I have even been accused of inventing some of these stories.

What I did, I took an old buggy, pulled the rubber tires off of it, took the tires off the rim and then I got hold of four of those hoop snakes. I tied these hoop snakes on instead of the tires and tied the wagon down to a stump there so it couldn't move. Finally I said, "Well, I'll give it a try." So I unhooked it from the stump and I got on the old buggy and boy, it just sat there spinning its wheels. I couldn't figure it out for a minute and then I looked and two of the wheels were going one way and the other two were going the other. What I'd done, I'd put two of them hoop snakes on backwards.

So, I took them off and I put them all headed the same way and made me a pretty good buggy. I had a horseless carriage there long before they ever had automobiles.

PARROT BIDDING

I spend most of my time up in this country, but once in a while I like to get down to the city and all and see how the other half lives. I was down there one day and saw a big sign there that says there's an auction and I like to go to auctions. So, I went to the auction and there in a big old cage was a great big old parrot. Boy, he was a magnificent looking bird and I liked him. They were going to auction him off so I made a bid there. I said "$20," and someone said "$30," Then I said "$40" and someone said "$50." Well, it kept going up and up and finally it got up to my bid of $150 on that bird and the auctioneer said, "Going, going, gone!"

So I had got the parrot. I went over and picked up the cage with the bird in it and looked in there and I said, "Boy, I spent enough for you. I sure hope you can talk."

And the parrot said, "Talk! I guess I can talk! Who do you think was bidding against you?"

Knack with transitions sets Harvey apart from other good talkers swapping lies. "Working in the Woods" is the bridge from jokes and marvels to autobiographical tall tales. The vignette plays with quantity, time, and fixed meaning until the predictable — isn't. (One joke was a personal delight because my dad, an East Texas native ten years Harvey's senior, liked to drive late, sleep a few hours in a motel, and get back on the road. Waking up before dawn in post-war "tourist courts," he always yawned, "Well, it didn't take long to stay all night here!")

Woodsmen's yarns often turn on a test of wit or courage. Dick Richards, master liar, singer, dance caller, and musician from Lake Luzerne, remembers staying part of one night in a haunted house with Ken Bonner, the well-known woodsman and fiddler who is himself the subject of some amazing accounts. When men live and work together, conflicts between boss and crew are very personal. Embroidered yarns about contests of wit can defuse what might otherwise explode.

A deft transition brings us home to the skunks who tricked the trickster, and to Harvey carving his wooden chains.

WORKING IN THE WOODS

I did quite a lot of working in the woods up in this country. In fact, I worked up on Dunbrook Mountain three years one summer. It was a pretty good life, fresh air and exercise, regular sleep and lots of food. Boy, in the lumber camps they really feed you good, porkchops piled up two feet high on each plate and you could eat all you want. It was a good life. Hard work, though.

One camp, I didn't stay too long. The boss looked at me and he said, "Can you cut logs?" and I said, "Yeah, I sure can."

"Well," he said, "you go up in the woods and cut down a bunch of those trees there."

So I went up and cut down a bunch of the trees and I came down for dinner and said, "Hey boss, I got them cut down. What do you want me to do now?"

"Well," he said, "Did you cut them up?"

I said. "No, you told me to cut them down."

"Well, you should have cut them up, too."

And I said, "Well, you should make up your mind."

I was kind of a greenhorn I guess. One problem we had was, you had to get up here, oh, you had to get up there way in the wee hours of

114

the morning—about 4:00 o'clock or so. It didn't take long to stay all night in that camp!

Anyway, I wasn't working out too well. The boss, he tried to keep me on. But finally he said, "Harvey, I don't know how in the world we'll get on without you, but next Monday morning we're going to try."

ME IN THE
HAUNTED HOUSE

A lot of strange things happen up in this country. One thing is the haunted house way up the road here. It was pretty well haunted, I guess. Well, we all got together there once and the boys got talking. They offered to chip in and round up ten dollars and give me that ten dollars if I would stay in that haunted house all night. That was right after I got fired up in the woods and I needed the money pretty bad so I said, "O.K., I'll tackle it."

Before dark I went up and got into the haunted house and I sat there. It wasn't too cold in there. I was getting along pretty good and it had gone on, oh, just about midnight when all of a sudden I heard a little rustle. I looked up and, well sir, there came a ghost. It came in through the wall just as though it wasn't there and, you know, I went right out through the other wall the same way.

SKUNKS IN THE CELLAR

You never know what's going to happen up here. Here a while ago on a nice warm day I had the cellar doors wide open and I was airing it out a little bit . After a while I went down, oh, it was dark there, and I was going to close the door. But when I looked, there was a doggone skunk down in the cellar. Well, you don't monkey around too much with a skunk, you know, they're pretty strong — strong smelling. I went back up into the house. I didn't know what to do about it.

Finally I called up an old-timer up the street here and I said, "Hey, I got a skunk in the cellar here. The door's open but he won't come out and I'm not about to go down in there and chase him out."

The old timer said, "I'll tell you what to do. You just put down a stream of honey. Boy, they like honey. Just like raccoons, they really like honey. You take some honey and you just pour a streak of honey right down as close as you dare get to him, right from there and right up to the stairway and right outside. Then," he said, "that skunk'll probably come out."

So, I got a jug of honey and I started and I poured it and I poured it down in and got as close as I dared to him. I had a good streak of

117

honey all the way into the yard. The next morning when I went to see how I'd made out — I'll be a son of a gun, there were two more skunks down the cellar! They liked honey too.

WOODEN CHAINS

There's a lot of different ways to make a living up here. There's lots of hobbies and a lot of things you can do for a passtime, and one of my passtimes is carving wooden chains. This is the truth. You probably don't believe me, but what you do is just take a stick of wood, say an inch square, or two inches square or whatever and six or eight or ten feet long, whatever, and you just carve yourself a wooden chain out of that piece of wood. It isn't too much of a job. It just takes quite a lot of time and quite a lot of patience — and quite a lot of bandaids till you get good at it.

So, I got a bunch of chains hanging around here, oh, about 55 feet of them. The beauty of it is, you can take a piece of wood, say an inch and a half square, and make it longer. I took that one piece there, that was exactly ten feet long. When I got all through with it, it was 12 feet, seven inches long, and that's the honest truth.

I'd like to demonstrate but you got to drop in, come up the house almost any old time. I'm pretty much at home now and the latch string is always out. If you want to stop and look at some chains I'll be glad to have you.

In fact, I got one of the chains up in a

museum now. They wanted one up there, lumberjack style. It is carved about the size of a log chain and that's up in the museum along with my jackknife and a couple of other little gadgets. In fact,they wanted me to stay up there. What they wanted to do, they wanted to stuff me and put me in a corner for an exhibit .

I said, "Only one way I'll go along with that. If you're gonna stuff me you'll have to stuff me with lobster and prime rib."

Well, that's pretty expensive stuff and they decided to forget about it.

If country people love confounding city people with mixed-up logic, what they love more is telling! The extravagant understatements, the apt metaphor for the terrible Adirondack top soil, the crazy inversions in "Hard Times" and in "Windmills and Log Cabins," illustrate the quiet pride in self-reliance and the lack of self-pity characteristic of woods people. "Maple Syrup" is a delicious sample of Yankee ingenuity. A logical inversion slips into the big one about north country spring weather. With characteristic lack of cruelty, Harvey doesn't make the teacher the butt of educated fellow jokes. Instead, schoolteacher Jim is Harvey's straight man for a poor man joke and a mixed-season impossibility. Best of all, the narrator in the numskull mask assigns the properties of one category to another. Or is it all an act to test the outsider?

HARD TIMES

Yeah, things were pretty rough up here years ago when I was a young fella. It was hard work, real hard work, but I liked it. I liked the fresh air and exercise. You got lots of both up here. I was up in there one day, up on Dunbrook Mountain sitting there, just sitting there looking around, when a guy came up through. I guess he was a hunter. He said he was, anyway. He said he was hunting for a place to fish.

Anyhow he said, "What are you doing up here?"

I said, "Well, I work up here."

He said, "You're not cutting any logs, I haven't heard your saw running or anything."

"No," I said, "Today's my day off."

WIND MILLS AND
LOG CABINS

You know, I liked it up there in the woods. It was hard work and all that but we had a little garden. We used to grow a little stuff there. Pretty tough trying to grow anything up there. In fact, you have to plant the corn with a shot gun. It's the only way you can get it into the ground.

We got by pretty well. We were quite resourceful. One thing we did, we built a couple of wind mills, put belts on them and used that wind power to cut logs or churn the butter or whatever you wanted to do. But we had to take one of the mills down because we didn't have wind enough for both.

Yes, we got along pretty good. Things could have been worse. I wasn't actually born in a log cabin or a little log shanty, but we moved into one as soon as we could afford it.

You know, there used to be an old fella up there years ago. I think he was kind of a story teller. He told me he lived in a log cabin and he was born in that log cabin. Not only that, he built it himself. I never could quite figure that out. I think he was quite windy and we could have used him when we had the windmills going.

MAPLE SYRUP

I'll tell you a little bit about our maple syrup project we had here two years ago. A buddy of mine and I, we made quite a lot of maple syrup. In fact, we made 235 gallons that year, and it took a lot of doing. You know, it takes about 30 or 35 gallons of sap to make one gallon of syrup, so you got to do a lot of boiling it down, a lot of evaporating there to make good syrup. There's a lot of work involved in it.

We had an old jeep there and we had a tank on the back of it. We'd go around to all the roadside trees and wherever we could get with the jeep. We'd dump the sap into that tank and haul it down to the sugar house and put it in the storage tank.

I came down the road there one day and I met the state troopers. They saw me in that old jeep so they turned around and pulled me over and said, "Can we see your licence?"

I said, "Sorry about that, I don't have a licence."

They said, "But how about registration on the jeep here?"

And I said, "I don't see any."

They said, "Do the lights work?"

And I said, "I don't know, I don't think so. I

don't need them anyhow cause I only drive in the daytime".

They said, "How's the horn?"

I tried it and I said, "Guess it don't work."

They said, "How's your brakes?"

I said, "Well, I haven't got very good brakes on it."

And finally, do you know what they did? They gave me a ticket for hauling sap without a vehicle.

Yeah, we made a lot of syrup, had a lot of fun. We had a pretty good spring there. We had good weather, more or less. We'd had a lot of stormy weather there, in March and April, but we didn't mind that too much. We were pretty well used to it.

But the one day there the wind came up and it started getting stronger and stronger. My buddy was out gathering sap or doing something. I was in the sugar shanty and I was boiling the sap. The wind came up and kept getting stronger and stronger. We had a ladder against the roof there and it blew that down. Then it blew the tank off the back of the jeep. Finally it got so windy there that it created an awful draft . Boy, that old fireplace that we boiled the sap on, man, did that get hot!

Well, of course we knew if it got too hot it'd burn the syrup. We started throwing in some wet green wood. Thought that would slow it down. But it burned that up just about as fast as we could throw it in there. In fact that draft got so strong there, it took chunks of wood right up through the chimney and right into the yard. They were all over the place. I had to go get them and bring them back.

Yeah, I had a friend with me there. This fella, he's a school teacher actually. He came up and helped us gather sap and so on and he kind of enjoyed it. He was helping me gather sap one day and he said, "How come you didn't tap those trees over there?".

"Well," I said, "we ain't got no more sap buckets."

Being a school teacher he looked at me kind of sharp and I said, "Jim, I know I'm not supposed to use a double negative and you're not supposed to say 'ain't,' but we just ain't got no more buckets."

One day there I pulled the old jeep up beside the road, kind of parked heading the wrong way, but it was a lot handier to get where the sap was, so I was parked headed the wrong way. There wasn't much traffic anyway.

Jim looked and said "Boy, you're on the wrong side of the road! Hope they don't give you a ticket for that." Then he said, "I'm glad I'm not driving. I got a real good record. I've driven a car for 40 years and never had a wreck."

I said, "Well, you know, Jim, I have a pretty good record too. I've driven a wreck for 40 years and never had a car."

Yeah, we had a lot of fun, lot of hard work, made a lot of syrup and we had a good time that spring. And it was getting around the end of the season here. Jim said, "Well, you like this syrup making, don't you?"

"You bet I do." I said. "You know as soon as I get the garden put in and the hay done, I'm going to come back and make some more syrup."

Grampa is the archetypal backwoodsman, the Crockett of the Central Adirondacks. He is the tough, remarkable man who never gets too excited. Especially, he isn't exercized about danger or pain. Even though Harvey's own grandfather was a "reckless old buzzard," Jack Roche was the model for Grampa. It all started after Jack came back to camp from a weekend at home.

"How'd things go?" Harvey asked.

"Not too good." Roche said, "My grandfather was in a bicycle race. He fell off and broke both legs." Harvey ". . . added to Jack's story and rebuilt it." Even with two broken legs, Grampa is well ahead of the book-educated doctor.

Grampa is a horse trader, the ultimate clever manipulator. The punch line for the final horse joke contains the word "half," which is the link of association for the next three nonsense clips. This tough old man ". . . in pretty good shape for his age," is the ideal in this culture. Youngsters who grow up hearing these stories understand that.

Like most of his contemporaries, Grampa is different among his cronies and at home. His wrangles with Gramma and with the woman next door are like the one he dropped into a telephone conversation:

> You gotta think things over. You know, God made earth and land and sea. . . He made man and then he took a rib from man and made woman. You know, there's times when I wish I had my rib back? I wouldn't dare say that except on the telephone!

Jokes like this are standard fare. Typically, the men who tell them marry for life, support their families,

128

and remain faithful. In context, these jokes relieve the tension and vent the frustration which is part of life-long commitment. Gramma, kicking Grampa under the table, keeps the upper hand. One thinks of those liars in Texas and Indiana, encouraged (by getting their toes stepped on) to pare the size of their lies. The wonderful deadpan brag about the old fellow's fast running is made bigger by Harvey's insistence that the problem is Grampa's annoyance at Harvey's teasing.

MORE ABOUT OL' GRAMPA

Well, I'll tell you a little more about Ol' Grampa. Quite a frisky old fella. He was in a bicycle race a while ago and he broke both legs and wound up in the hospital in a wheelchair. You know, he totaled four wheelchairs before they got the cast off him.

But he came out of it pretty good. He asked the doctor afterwards, "Hey, Doc, do you think I'll be able to dance the jig now?"

The doctor said, "Oh yes. You'll be able to."

And Grampa said, "Hey, that's great, I never could before."

Grampa was quite a busy little beaver. He always had to be doing something, even when he was laid up with those broken legs. So he started making stools. Well, he made all different kind of stools. But he had a little problem with them, trying to get all four legs to fit the floor at the same time. He'd start cutting them off. He'd cut this one off and try and he'd cut that one off and by the time he'd get it all done that stool wouldn't be more than three or four inches high.

He solved that, though. He quit making four-legged stools and went to making three-legged ones. You know, they would fit the floor no matter what shape it was in.

All of this was way back, back about the time Paul Bunyan was just a kid and Babe, the ox, was just a calf. Grampa had quite a lot of horses around at different times. He was a pretty sharp dealer when it came to horses. He had one horse and it had a problem, so he told this fella he wanted to sell it.

The fella asked, "What shape is that horse in"?

"He doesn't look good," Grampa said, "but he's healthy enough, he's strong and husky. The only thing he doesn't look very good."

So the guy said, "What do you want for him?"

"Well, a hundred dollars, I guess."

That was a good deal, so the fella gave Grampa a hundred dollars. He took that horse home, put him out in the field and started working with him. Before long, though, that fella came back madder than a wet cat.

He said, "Hey, you son of a gun, that horse is blind!"

"Well," my Grampa said, "I told you he didn't look very good."

Grampa had to take that horse back again. He was blind, but he wasn't a bad horse. He lived to a ripe old age and finally he died. Well Grampa being quite a horse trader anyhow, he kind of hated losing all that money so he decided to raffle him off. He made up a bunch of raffle tickets and he told folks he was raffling off a horse. He sold them all over the neighborhood and all over the countryside and had this raffle. It was a big success and Grampa made quite a bit of money.

I asked him about it afterward. I said, "Grampa, you raffled off a dead horse?"

He said, "Well, yeah."

I said, "Didn't you get in trouble when it turned out the horse was dead?"

He said, "No, not really."

"How come?"

"Well," he said. "the only guy that complained about it was the guy who won him and I gave him his money back."

Grampa had quite a time with his horses. He had a little problem now and then, though. He had this one horse that was quite a frisky. One day it hauled off and kicked Grampa right over, upended him.

Grampa rolled right across the yard. Gramma looked out the window and she could see that Grampa was kind of hurt . So she ran right over to the phone and she called the doctor.

"Oh doctor, oh doctor," she said, "come quick! Come right over here. The horse just kicked my husband."

The doctor said, "Where did it kick him?"

Gramma thought about that for a minute,

132

"Well," she finally said, "just about halfway between the post and the barn."

Back in the depression time there, times were pretty hard and good food was pretty hard to come by. So what Grampa did, he went out and he hunted rabbits a lot. It was legal then to sell game. So he'd hunt the rabbits, shoot them, take them and sell them to people whole. Sometimes he'd dress them out and just sell the meat.

It went along good at first. But after a while Grampa had hunted so many rabbits they were getting kind of scarce. So he decided to mix in a little horse meat. That sold good, so he kept putting in a little more horse meat and a little more horse meat and a little more horse meat. Finally some of the people that were buying this meat from him got wind of it and they started to complain a little bit.

So the sheriff came over to see him.

The sheriff said, "Hey, just what"s going on here? They tell me you're putting horse meat in with the rabbit meat."

"Well," Grampa said, " I have been putting in some."

The sheriff said, "Well, how much have you been putting in?"

"Well," Grampa said, "I've been mixing it up just about half and half."

The sheriff said, "Half and half?"

Grampa said, "Ye-up, one horse to one rabbit."

Grampa had quite an imagination. He even made up his own mixed drink. He called it the Senior Citizen Cocktail.

I asked him, "Grampa, how do you mix them up?"

He said "Half and half."

And I said. "Half and half what?"

He said, "Half gin and half Geritol."

I guess it worked good because he seemed to be in pretty good shape for his age.

Quite an old boy, Ol' Grampa there. A little bit stingy maybe, but times were pretty hard, and money was pretty scarce and it took quite a bit of doing just to make a half-way decent living.

Gramma, though, had always wanted a nice fur. She wanted a mink coat.

But Grampa said, "No, we can't afford it."

Well, times got a little better and Gramma asked him again.

Once again Grampa said, "Nope, can't afford it."

By now, Gramma was getting kind of impatient. Times had gotten pretty good, but she still didn't have that fur coat. Finally she said, "Aren't you ever going to get me a mink coat?"

He said, "Nope, guess not."

She said, "Give me one good reason".

He said. "Well, the way I look at it, if Mother Nature wanted you to have a fur coat she would have given you one."

But times got better and better, and Grampa

got to the point where he was making pretty good money. So, finally Gramma got her fur coat, a nice mink coat.

The next door neighbor lady came over and she was looking it all over. She said, "That's a beautiful coat. I wish I had one of them. I bet that keeps you warm."

Grampa said, "Well, didn't rightly get it to keep her warm. I got it to keep her quiet!"

I guess it worked out pretty good because Gramma used to talk about how stingy Grampa was. He wouldn't buy this and he wouldn't buy that. One day Gramma said, "You know, Grampa is so stingy, he wouldn't give a nickel to see a grasshopper eat a bale of hay."

But after she got her mink coat she didn't say anything more about his being stingy.

Grampa didn't get along with that next-door lady. One day when she visited she said to Gramma, "You know I been married three times. But my husbands, all three of them died."

Grampa said, "I couldn't say that I blame them much." He was always getting in hassles with that next-door lady and one day she got pretty peeved at him. She said, "You know, if you were my husband I'd put poison in your food."

He said, "Well sir, if you were my wife I would surely eat it."

Grampa used to be quite a storyteller himself. I don't know if that's where I picked up some of my stories, or if it's in our blood or something but he used to tell some pretty tall stories. When they had company, Grampa and Gramma would sit at the table after dinner and visit for a while. Sooner or later, Grampa would be telling those big stories. But if he started to exaggerate too much, Gramma would kick him one under the table.

One day, he was telling company about this big haystack that he made. "That haystack," he said, "was five hundred fifty long and it was two hundred feet wide."

Just then Gramma kicked him under the table.

"Well," he said, "it was only two feet high."

Grampa had a pretty good sense of humor for an old boy there and he was a lot of fun. He got peeved once,, though, when something happened that I thought was funny but he didn't. What happened was he got stuck with a wagonload of wood. The horses weren't pulling, so he got on top of the load and took out his whip and he hollered, "Get, get!"

Well, when they got, well they lunged so hard that they broke off the plank that holds the horses to the wagon. They broke that plank right off and away went the horses. Well, Grampa was hanging right onto the lines and he went with them. He was pretty spry, so when they pulled him off of the wagon he landed on his feet and started running to keep up to them, trying to slow them down. Man, they were really going. When I see him coming, they were going along it looked like 40 miles an hour or so.

So, I stood there and here come the team with Grampa running along behind them hanging onto the lines.

I hollered, "Hey Grampa, you forgot the wagon."

You know, Grampa didn't think that was very funny.

One day I said "Grampa, how old do you have to be before you quit chasing women?"

"Well sir," he said, "I'll tell you, you're going to have to ask somebody older than I am."

Some dogs, and some masters, can be rigid fools who follow commands to absurdity. The story about the paralyzed pointer, which also is found among rural black hunters in Alabama and Louisiana, is an illogical, logical consequence of exact obedience, and (since the prey was also paralyzed) of sympathetic magic. Smart dogs speak in sign language. They outsmart rabbit, flea, deer—and master! Harvey's lineage has ". . . quite a bit of Irisher," so it isn't surprising that a story about a fox ridding himself of fleas in a stream has been collected in Ireland.

If Harvey identifies with his dogs, he sympathizes with the other creatures. He "believes one hundred per cent that animals have personality." One thinks of Aesop, of Irish hero tales, of St. Francis—gone comic.

138

MORE ABOUT SPARKY

Maybe I'll tell you a little more about my old dog Sparky. She is quite a dog, she is. I have a lot of fun with her. Well, she was kind of a tough little dog to get along with when she was a puppy, but I did find out one thing. When you've got a little puppy dog around and you're going to buy socks you better buy a dozen pair all the same color. Cause puppies have a habit of chewing up one sock of each color, and then you can't get your socks to match.

Ol' Sparky likes to play cards with me. She is not too bad at it. She is pretty good at cribbage and rummy, but she's not much good at playing poker because when she gets good hands she always wags her tail.

Yeah, she is quite a dog, good Ol' Sparky. She isn't really a rabbit hound and she isn't a beagle. She isn't even a hound. She is just a plain old friendly dog of mine. But she likes to chase rabbits. She can't follow their trail too well by their scent, but if she sees one, boy she takes after it and away they go, around, around, around. Of course, you know those rabbits, cottontails or snowshoes, either one, they always run in circles.

Well, what Sparky would do, she'd take after them and get chasing them. They'd start around in circles, and she would get going like lightning, going around in circles there, and then she'd stop and wait till the next time they came around and she'd get em.

She's a pretty smart old dog in some ways. I had quite a time with there when she got fleas. Boy, she had a lot of them. I was sure I would to have to take her to the vet and get her sprayed or get something done to her. But before I took her to the vet, I took her down and went fishing. She always liked to go with me. I went down fishing down to Blue Mountain Lake here and I baited up and I started fishing and I looked around and there's Old Sparky in the water with a big old stick in her mouth. She was just swimming around, and around with that stick in her mouth and not paying any attention to me and I couldn't figure out what she was up too. Just her nose and that stick sticking out of the water. After a while, I looked closer to see what was happening. Those fleas on Sparky were down under water and they were drowning, so they were all coming up and on to that stick. As soon as all the fleas got on that stick, Ol' Sparky let go and away went the stick, fleas and all.

Yeah, I used to take Ol' Sparky about everywhere I went. I even took her deer hunting. I trained her so she wouldn't chase deer, cause that would be illegal if she was chasing deer.

140

But what I would do was to go out on a nice warm, sunny day, and set up against a tree. Ol' Sparky would set there with me. At first, if she saw a deer, she would bark. That scared the deer and I didn't want that. So I trained her so that if she saw a deer, she would just nip me a little bit, not enough to hurt me, just enough to wake me up. I could go to sleep and if she saw deer she would just reach over real slow and gentle like, and she'd nip me a little bit and I'd wake up and look around and sure enough there'd be some deer.

She was kind of a funny-looking dog though. Her regular color, she's kind of a dark tan and partly white and in deer season she looked a little bit too much like a deer. So what I did, I spray-painted her bright red with food coloring. That made kind of a funny-looking dog out of her but she was a lot safer that way and it wore off soon after deer season.

Used to have quite a time with Ol' Sparky in hot weather. Soon as the cold weather and winter was over and spring come along and it got pretty warm, boy, she would start to shed. She shed like crazy! She's got kind of long silky hair and it just came off of her and being almost white, it stuck to everything. You could see it for a half a mile.

So I brushed off quite a lot of it, about a shopping bag full of hair every time I brushed her. It was pretty good silk-looking hair, so I took it to a woman who had some sheep there and spun her own wool. She looked at it and said she could spin it. So she spun a whole bunch of it into wool, and I took it home and I had my good wife Mary knit a sweater out of it just about Sparky's size. And golly, it fit pretty good.

It really worked out good because Sparky didn't need that hair in the warm weather anyway and it came in real handy in cold weather. Nowadays she wears her little old sweater in the cold weather and then in the warm weather we just take it off and put it away and she doesn't have to shed anymore. It works out real good.

Yeah, Ol' Sparky is a great dog to have around, a lot of company. But she's kind of a nuisance sometimes. When I take her fishing she likes to go with me, but she jumps around and splashes in the water. What's more, she uses the wrong type of bait and she gets her hooks snarled up in the trees. It seems that she does everything wrong. Worst part, though, is that she catches more fish than I do.

A REAL GOOD POINTER

Yeah, I used to have another dog there. She was an English setter and boy, she was a real good pointer. She'd track down a pheasant and when she got its scent she'd freeze. You'd see her freeze right in position there with one foot up and she would stay right there till I was ready. I'd say, "get'um!" and she'd run ahead and flush that pheasant.

Well, I was out one day, up Lake Ontario country there. It was awful brushy — tag alders and a lot of brush up there. I took her hunting and we got along pretty good. I guess we got a couple of pheasants. Then she took off down into that thicket, a regular little jungle. No way I could get in there. I waited and waited and waited. I didn't see her and didn't hear any pheasants go out of there or anything and I didn't know just what the problem was. Well, I waited and I waited and finally I had to go home. I left my jacket there so if she came out she would lay on my jacket.

I left the jacket there three or four days. Each time I went back I'd call for her and look around real good and I never did find her. Finally, I had to get another dog.

Well, a couple of years later I was out with the other dog. It was another English setter and

143

I was right in the same area. I went through some brush and there was the skeleton of my dog just standing there. Just a skeleton with one foot up and standing right there with her nose up. So I walked up ahead about 50 to 75 feet and there was the skeleton of a pheasant.

PRETTY GOOD ON PARTRIDGE

That one old dog I had was quite a bird dog, quite a good one. Pretty good on partridge. We'd go out hunting and she'd be up ahead of me looking around real careful-like. I'd watch her real close and then all of a sudden she'd stop and I'd stop.

Well, what she'd do if there was one partridge in there she'd hold up one foot. If there were two partridges in there she'd hold up two feet and if she saw three partridge in there she'd hold up three feet.

One time, though, she reached over and grabbed a stick and shook the daylights out of it. I couldn't figure out for quite a while what she meant. Finally, it came to me. What she was trying to tell me was that there were more partridge in there than you can shake a stick at.

Our hero is on a bewitched flight — with a tall tale twist! The magic air journey is a universal symbol for the escape from the world of ordinary routine to a realm of miracle. It is a metaphor for what the artist sees.

There is a way, for me, that this story stands for Harvey's art. It all begins very normally, at home. He goes on a journey to gather materials to build what he has pictured. He speeds up, starts to play with extremes. Suddenly, transported by speed and wind, he is airborne — looking down on his world, seeing it in a larger frame. Unlike some characters in flight tales (Dorothy on her way to Oz, for example), Harvey never loses control. By working with the situation, he manages to keep his direction, and to come back to earth without ". . . a bit of trouble." Comedy is about managed perspective, about seeing human life as just that.

FLYING PLYWOOD

One day I was doing some work here. I was kind of putting things together in a hurry and I ran out of plywood. I needed just one more sheet, a 4' by 8' piece of plywood. So, I went down to Indian Lake, that's about 11 miles from here and I got that piece of plywood. I didn't have a truck. All I had was my car, so I tied that plywood on top of the car, hopped in and started for home.

I wanted to finish that job that day and I was in a pretty good hurry, so I stepped on it pretty good. I think maybe my speedometer was running over a little bit, but I was making good time and I was getting along good. Well, I was coming west there to Blue Mountain Lake when there came a pretty strong west wind and I drove right into it. Well, that wind got in under that plywood and up I went, car and all, right up in the air. I was up there 10 to 12 feet above the road. I was in a real pickle then because it was quite a job trying to steer the car. You know, I couldn't get the front wheels to do anything for me cause they weren't on the ground. I was staying right side up, but I was getting a little worried. I was afraid we were going to land in the middle of the lake. Then I discovered that if I hung onto the steering wheel real careful-like and then leaned one way or the other I could steer that plywood and my car. So I steered it right around and finally got it back up pretty near Blue Mountain Lake and I eased back on the gas and I landed right in the road without a bit of trouble. But I slowed down a bit after that.

The ice fishing pun? Harvey can't help himself. Jokes about priests are a regular feature in French Canadian woods humor. The story about the priest who plans to plant pickled watermelon seeds cross-breeds a literal-minded numskull with a drunken cleric. The re-setting of the Texas jokes, giving our hero the last possible word, echoes a story collected in the Catskills in which an American is contemptuous of the size of things in England. The Englishman, who has had enough, puts six large lobsters in the American's bed. When the American asks what they are, the Englishman replies, "Bed bugs."

Harvey brings us home from our magic journey and sets us down. Easy.

ICE FISHING

I used to do almost anything up here that was kind of legal-like to make a living. Somebody had told me about ice fishing and I thought that sounded pretty good and I asked them how to do it.

"Well," they said, " you go out in the middle of the lake and find a good level spot and you chop a hole in the ice and you go just ice fishing."

I thought I understood just what he was talking about. So, I went out one day and I chopped a hole in the ice and I chopped and chopped and chopped and I stayed there for a while doing pretty good — or so I thought I had one of those five gallon plastic pails and before long I got it right chuck full of ice!

Well, I carried it back and Mary said, "What did you bring all that home for? We got all the ice we can use here now."

The only trouble with that ice fishing is when you need the ice in the summer, there ain't no ice there. So I quit ice fishing.

WOOD KEEPS YOU WARM IN A LOT OF WAYS

Used to cut a lot of wood to make a living. I'd cut it, pile it and sell it and I had a pretty good sale stock lined up there. Now wood really keeps you warm. I learned that the hard way. It keeps you warm when you cut it, it keeps you warm when you split it, keeps you warm when you bring it out to the road, and when you put it in the stove. And when you're taking it out and hauling the ashes, it really keeps you warm!

When times got a little better there, a salesman came through and selling oil-fed heaters. Everybody told me about these oil heaters. They burn steady all night and you didn't have to put wood in or anything, so it's pretty handy. He sold me one with a built-in hot water system and he said, "That's just the one you need. Not only will it keep you nice and warm in the winter, it'll keep you in hot water all the while you're paying for it."

I'M 53 YEARS OLD

Maybe, I'll tell you a little more about me. Naturally, I'm 53 years old and a few months. A fella asked me the other day how many months, and I said, "Well, about 243 of them, I guess"

I'm pretty healthy for the shape I'm in and I've had a pretty good life, but I did get pretty fat there for a while. Then I saw an ad in the paper. It said, **Get these diet pills and lose all the weight you want.** So I got the information and they said they'd send me a month's supply of diet pills and they'd guarantee I'd lose. I was to send them $35.00. So, I sent them the $35.00 and back came the pills. You know, I gained two pounds, but I did lose something. I lost $35.00.

Yeah, I used to have quite an appetite. I could eat just about anything in sight if it was edible. I finally went to the doctor on day and asked him if he would give me some pills to take. I was weighing pretty heavy there. He looked me over and he said, "Now here, you take these pills and you take two of them after each meal but not over twelve pills a day."
It was kind of hard to figure that out, because I ate a lot more often than that.

PRIEST PICKLED WATERMELON

I used to do quite a bit of experimenting with food and cooking up stuff and so on and I came up with one mixture, one concoction there I thought was pretty good. What it was, was pickled watermelon. You just cut the watermelon up in chunks and put it in a pickle barrel. I had this special brine that I put it in and pickled them in that. Well, I lost the recipe for the brine and I didn't know what to do. But I did have a big old jug of brandy there. So, I said to myself, well I'll try that, it's all I've got. I pickled a bunch of that watermelon in the brandy. It had been pickled for a while and it came Sunday and we had the priest here to have dinner with us and Mary, she said right in the middle of the meal, she said, "Oh my Lord, I forgot to make dessert."

"Well," I said, "what we can do, is we can have some of that pickled watermelon."

Mary kind of looked at me. She knew they were pickled in brandy, but we had the pickled watermelon for dessert. It went over pretty good and we had a nice dinner and a nice visit and after the priest left, Mary said "Harvey, you think the priest liked the pickled watermelon?"

"I'm pretty doggone sure he did. After he ate all the watermelon he put the seeds in his pocket."

UNCLES OUT WEST

Oh, I got to tell you about this fella I was talking with from out west. He came to New York State and he was working up in the lumber camp there with me. He said, "I'm from Minnesota. My uncle is still out there. My uncle, he's a big man. He is a strong man. A great big, strong man. He takes two logs and rubs them together . . . sawdust."

I said, "Well, you know, I got an uncle out west too. He's down in Arizona and he's a rancher. He got a great big ranch, takes you four days to drive across it. He's got a lot of cattle there and he is a big man, oh, he's a strong man. He just takes two bulls and rubs them together . . . baloney."

Had another fella sat there listening to us and he said, "Yeah, I got an uncle out west too, he's down in Texas. Been in Texas quite a while there now."

So I says, "How many acres does he own?"

"Well, quite a lot," he said, "about 500 acres."

And I said, "500 acres? You call that a lot of land?"

"Well," he said, "that's in downtown Fort Worth."

We had another guy from Texas and he was

telling how big the state of Texas was. He said, "You know, if you take the state of Texas, you put a hinge right on the upper end of it, up on the north end of Texas, and take hold of the south end and tip it up, you can tip it right up so it would reach to the Canadian border."

And I said, "Man, oh man, you wouldn't want to do that. You Texans would freeze to death up there."

This buddy of mine from Texas, he came up to see me a while back. Everything is big down there. The trees are big, the cattle are all big, the ranches are big and everything is big. So I thought I'd have a little fun with him. I went down to the swamp down here and I got three or four snapping turtles. I brought them up and when he wasn't looking I rolled the sheets back on his bed, put them in there, put the sheets right back in place and went down. We had the evening together. Then he went up to go to bed and I listened. All of a sudden a terrible screech came out of him.

"What in the world is going on around here?" he yelled.

So I went up and I said, "Ronnie, what's the matter, what's the matter?"

He said, "Look at that, that son of a gun had me by the toe. What is it?"

"Well," I said, "that's an Adirondack bed bug."

He took another look at it and "I'll be a son of a gun" he said. "A young one, isn't it?"

156

SO LONG, ETC.

Well, I guess that's all the tape I got, kinda running out of stories, experiences, whatever you want to call them. But I've had a good time enjoying all these experiences and I had a pretty good time talking about them. And if you don't believe me, I can't rightly say that I blame you a bit. I don't really intend to lie but once in a while, as they say about old liars, old liars never die they just get carried away.

These stories were transcribed just as Harvey told them from a tape — actually, a radio show complete with sound effects — early in the spring of 1991.

Jim Meehan, media curator at the Adirondack Museum, was very generous in helping me to understand how Harvey's storytelling works at home. Bob Bethke, my favorite oral tradition expert, has worked at some length with Harvey Carr. I have learned a great deal from watching Bob work, and from what he has had to say in our all-too-occasional conversations.

SELECTED
BIBLIOGRAPHY

The Adirondacks

Bruchac, Joseph, Craig Hancock, Alice Gilborn, and Jean Rickoff. *North Country: An Anthology of Contemporary Writing from the Adirondacks and the Upper Hudson Valley*. Greenfield Center, N.Y.: Greenfield Review Press, 1986.

Bethke, Robert D. *Adirondack Voices: Woodsmen and Woods Lore*. Chicago: University of Illinois Press, 1981.

Bethke, Robert D., and Varick Chittenden. *Speaking of the North Country: A Northern New York Oral Storytelling Sampler*. Canton, N.Y.: St. Lawrence County Historical Association, 1989.

Conklin, Henry. *Through Poverty's Vale: A Hardscrabble Boyhood in Upstate New York, 1832–1862*. Syracuse: Syracuse University Press, 1974.

Donaldson, Alfred L. *A History of the Adirondacks*. New York: Century Publishing Company, 1921. Two volume reprint, Harrison, New York: Harbor Hill Books, 1977. Introduction and biographical sketch by John J. Duquette.

Fowke, Edith. *Lumbering Songs from the Northern Woods*. Austin: University of Texas Press, 1970.

Hammod, S.H. *Wild Northern Scenes, or Sporting Adventures with the Rifle and Rod*. New York: Derby and Jackson, 1857.

Headley, J.T. *Letters from the Backwoods and the Adirondac*. New York: John S. Taylor, 1850.

Hochschild, Harol K. *Lumberjacks and Rivermen in the*

161

Central Adirondacks: 1850–1950. Blue Mountain Lake, N.Y.: Adirondack Museum, 1962.

Jamieson, Paul F. *The Adirondack Reader*.

Keith, Herbert F. *Man of the Woods*. Syracuse: Syracuse University Press, 1972.

Radford, Harry V. *Adirondack Murray*. New York: Broadway Publishing Company, 1905.

Roberts, Jesse David. *Bears, Bibles, and a Boy*. New York: W.W. Norton, 1961.

Smith, H. Perry. *The Modern Babes in the Woods, or Summerings in the Wilderness*. Hartford: Columbian Book Co., 1872.

Street, Alfred B. *Woods and Waters, or the Saranac and Racket*. New York: M. Doolady, 1860. Reprint: Harrison, N.Y.: Harbor Hill Books, 1976.

Sylvester, Nathaniel. *Historical Sketches of Northern New York and the Adirondack Wilderness*. Troy, N.Y.: William H. Young, 1877. Reprint: Harbor Hill Books, 1973.

Stoddard, Seneca Ray. *Old Times in the Adirondacks: The Narrative of a Trip into the Wilderness, 1873*. Edited by Maitland DeSormo. Saranac Lake, N.Y.: Maitland DeSormo, 1971.

Thomas, Howard. *Tales from the Adirondack Foothills*. Prospect, N.Y.: Prospect Books, 1967.

Williams, Donald R. *Oliver H. Whitman, Adirondack Guide, and Other Adirondack Stories Based on the 1882–1920 Journals of Oliver Whitman*. Wells, N.Y.: Adirondack Books, 1979.

Warner, Anne. *Traditional American Folk Songs from the Anne and Frank Warner Collection*. "New York State," pp. 38–122. Syracuse: Syracuse University Press, 1984.

Tall Tale

Allen, Ethan. *A Narrative of Col Allen's Captivity*. Walpole, N.H.: Thomas and Thomas, 1807.

162

Aswell, James R., et al. *God Bless the Devil! Liars' Bench Tales*. Reprint: Knoxville: University of Tennessee Press, 1985.

Austin, William. *A Book of New England Legends by Samuel Adams Drake*. Boston: Roberts Brothers, 1884.

Audobon, John James. *Ornithological Biography, Vol. I*. Philadelphia: Judah Dobson, 1831.

Bruchac, Joseph. *Hoop Snakes, Hide-Behinds and Sidehill Winders*. Freedom, Ca.: The Crossing Press, 1991.

Cutting, Edith E. *Lore of an Adirondack County*. Ithaca, N.Y.: Cornell University Press, 1944.

Davidson, Sargeat Bull. *Tall Tales They Tell in the Service*. New York: Thomas Y. Crowell Co., 1943.

Gardner, Emelyn Elizabeth. *Folklore from the Schoharie Hills, New York*. Ann Arbor: University of Michigan Press, 1937.

Lofuro, Michael A. *The Tall Tales of Davy Crockett: The Second Nashville Series of Crockett Almanacs (1839–1841)*. Knoxville: University of Tennessee Press, 1987.

Studer, Norman. "Yarns of a Catskill Woodsman." *New York Folklore Quarterly* (1955), 183–192.

Thompson, Harold. *Body, Boots, and Britches: Folktales, Ballads and Speech from Country New York*, 1939. Reprint: New York: Dover Books, 1967.

Welsh, Roger. *Catfish at the Pump: Humor and the Frontier*. Lincoln, Nebraska: Plains Heritage, 1982.

_____. *Shingling the Fog and Other Plains Lies*. Chicago: Swallow Press, 1972.

Folklore Analysis

Aarne, Antii. *The Types of the Folktale: A Classification and Bibliography*. Translated by Stith Thompson. New York: Burt Franklin, 1971.

Baughman, Ernest W. *Type and Motif Index of the Folk-*

tales of New England and North America. The Hague: Mouton and Company, 1966.

Blair, Walter. *Horse Sense in American Humor from Benjamin Franklin to Ogden Nash*. Chicago: University of Chicago Press, 1942.

_____. *Native American Humor*. New York: American Book Company, 1937.

Bauman, Richard. "Differential Identity and the Social Base of Folklore." *Journal of American Folklore*, 84, January–March 1971, 31–41.

Beaver, J. Russell. "From Reality to Fantasy: Opening-Closing Formulas in the Structures of American Tall Tales." *Southern Folkore Quarterly*, 36. 1972, 369–382.

Boatwright, Mody. *Folk Laughter on the American Frontier*. New York: Macmillan, 1949; Collier Books, 1961.

Brown, Carolyn S. *The Tall Tale in American Folkore and Literature*. Knoxville: University of Tennessee Press, 1987.

Corrigan, Robert W. "Comedy and the Comic Spirit," in *Comedy: Meaning and Form*. Scranton: Chandler Publishing Company, 1965, 18–60.

Dorson, Richard M. *Man and Beast in Comic Legend*. Bloomington: Indiana University Press, 1982.

Georges, Robert. "Towards an Understanding of Storytelling Events." *Journal of American Folklore*, 57. 1944, 97–106.

Harpman, Geoffrey Galt. *On the Grotesque: Strategies of Contradiction in Art and Literature*. Princeton: Princeton University Press, 1982.

Ives, Edward D. *Larry Gorman: The Man Who Made the Songs*. Bloomington: Indiana University Press, 1964.

_____. *Joe Scott: The Woodsman-Songmaker*. Chicago: University of Illinois Press, 1978.

Kenney, W. Howland. *Laughter in the Wilderness: Early American Humor to 1783*. Kent, Ohio: Kent State University Press, 1976.

Langer, Suzanne. "The Comic Rhythm." *Feeling and Form*. New York: Charles Scribner's Sons, 1953, 326–350.

Loomis, C. Grant. "The Tall Tale and the Miraculous." *California Folkore Quarterly*, 4. 1945, 109–128.

Masterson, James R. "Travelers' Tales of Colonial Natural History." *Journal of American Folklore*, 59, 1946, 174–188.

O'Suilleabhain, Sean. *A Handbook of Irish Folklore*. Dublin: The Folklore of Ireland Society, 1942.

Roberts, Warren. "The Art of Perpendicular Lying." *Journal of the Folklore Institute*, 2, 1965, 180–219.

Rourke, Constance. *American Humor: A Study of the National Character*. 1931. Reprint: New York: Harcourt, Brace, and Jovanovich, 1959.

Ryle, Gilbert. *The Concept of Mind*. New York: Barnes and Noble, 1950.

Sypher, Wylie. "The Meaning of Comedy." *Comedy: Meaning and Form*. Robert W. Corrigan, ed. Scranton: Chandler Publishing Co., 1965, 18–60.

Thompson, Stith. *The Folktale*, 1946. Reprint: Berkley: University of California Press, 1977.

Tolken, Barre. *The Dynamics of Folklore*. Boston: Houghton Mifflin, 1979.

Vansina, Jan. *Oral Tradition as History*. Madison: University of Wisconsin, 1965.

Welsford, Enid. *The Fool: His Social and Literary History*. London: Faber and Faber, 1935

ABOUT THE EDITOR

Vaughn Ramsey Ward has been collecting, performing, and presenting the traditions of the Lower Adirondack region for twenty years. She is a graduate of the University of New Mexico, where she studied music, art history, and English, and of the Bread Loaf School of English, Middlebury College, Vermont. She studied American Folk Culture at the Cooperstown Graduate Program of the State University of New York at Oneonta. Mrs. Ward has taught English, humanities, and folklore in high school and in college. Currently the staff folklorist for the Lower Adirondack Regional Arts Council in Glens Falls, New York, she is also the editor of I ALWAYS TELL THE TRUTH (EVEN IF I HAVE TO LIE TO DO IT!): TALES FROM THE ADIRONDACK LIARS' CLUB, which was published in 1990 by the Greenfield Review Press and selected for the American Library Association's *Recommended List*.

HARVEY CARR
1917–1991